TERRORDOME

Nicola Ralph

dizzyemupublishing.com

DIZZY EMU PUBLISHING

1714 N McCadden Place, Hollywood, Los Angeles 90028

dizzyemupublishing.com

Terrordome
Nicola Ralph

First published in the United States
in 2022 by Dizzy Emu Publishing

Copyright © Nicola Ralph 2022

Nicola Ralph has asserted her right under the
Copyright, Designs and Patents Act 1988 to be
identified as the author of this work.

1 3 5 7 9 10 8 6 4 2

dizzyemupublishing.com

TERRORDOME

Nicola Ralph

<u>TERRORDOME</u>

Written by

Nicola Ralph

Terrordome

AN ELECTRICAL HUM.

A blur of color and movement.

PIXELS, up close - We MOVE OUT - the image comes into view -

EXT. CITY STREET, THE DOME (ESPORTS INDOOR STADIUM) - DUSK

A massive dark structure, striking against the vibrant city lights on the skyline. Drawing the eye like a black hole pulls in light.

We see it on a camera's digital screen as someone SNAPS a shot amongst the HORDE OF PEOPLE heading towards it.

FROM ABOVE we see surrounding roads are grid-locked. The thousands on foot head in the same direction - toward the imposing structure.

MONTAGE - INT./EXT. DOME - NIGHT

A) A line of TICKET HOLDERS snakes as far as the eye can see.

                    FEMALE REPORTER (O.S.)
          Its opening night for the World's
          largest ever custom built Esports
          stadium, courtesy of gaming mogul
          and household name Tom Niko and one
          of the most anticipated events in
          the history of entertainment.

B) GAMING FANS enter the stadium.

SECURITY check for contraband via floor to ceiling scanning screens that HIGHLIGHT OBJECTS from knives (and guns) to liquor, even bra underwire and braces.

                    FEMALE REPORTER (O.S.) (CONT'D)
          Not only is this the unveiling of
          this magnificent feat in state-of-
          the-art architectural wonder, it is
          the first public demonstration of
          Mr. Niko's newest and most exciting
          virtual reality console *and* the
          launch of its first game, the long-
          awaited 'Alien Abduction: Endless
          Terror'. Its true what they say,
          three really is the magic number.

Security stop and frisk only those with prohibited objects as if psychic!

- A knife is found on a WHITE MAN as TWO BLACK MEN pass untouched, gawking.

- A SWEET-LOOKING WOMAN is found to possess cocaine.

C) The WORLD'S MEDIA in and around the STADIUM cover every angle.

>   FEMALE REPORTER (O.S.) (CONT'D)
>   For the first time ever players
>   will really *feel* the world of the
>   game in this fully immersive gaming
>   experience, expected to soon become
>   the future norm of entertainment.

D) Bottlenecked CROWDS enter the MAIN AUDITORIUM taking their seats and gradually filling the stadium.

>   FEMALE REPORTER (O.S.) (CONT'D)
>   Top non-professional online gamers
>   have been selected to take part in
>   the live demonstration in front of
>   50,000 spectators.

E) MERCH AREAS are veiled in mystery - nothing on show. Instead, people enter small individual cubicles - coming out with bags of merchandise.

>   FEMALE REPORTER (O.S.) (CONT'D)
>   Still miraculously shrouded in
>   mystery, what *is* known is this
>   event is sure to go down in gaming
>   history.

F) The FEMALE REPORTER direct to camera -

>   FEMALE REPORTER (O.S.) (CONT'D)
>   And it all starts right here at the
>   stroke of midnight.
>   (to Cameraman)
>   Was that better?

>   CUT TO BLACK:

OPENING CREDITS

SUPER: THE DAY BEFORE THE LAUNCH

INT. EXTRAVAGANT HOTEL ENTRANCE/FOYER - DAY

Flustered, MARCUS GORDON (21, Black) enters the grand, bustling hotel - intimidated and in awe. He observes those around him as he tries to get his bearings (we will see more of these people later) -

Bespectacled gamer THIRTEEN, rummages in his bag at the desk.

                    THIRTEEN
          I just had it at the airport.

Young professional, hipster-types cross paths - Gamer ONE,
bearded, early-thirties, and gamer THREE, handsome, mid-
twenties -

                    ONE
          See you in 30.

                    THREE
          For sure.

Frank-talking New Yorker LARA, 19, white, approaches a gentle
giant of a man in his fifties (SIX) -

                    LARA
          Hey, is this the line for check-in?

                    SIX
          It is.

A baby-faced KID (gamer Nineteen) with his late-thirties
father join the line behind Lara. Marcus finally decides to
get in line behind them -

                    KID
          What if they ask for ID?

                    KID'S DAD
          Leave it to me.

INT. EXTRAVAGANT HOTEL FOYER NEAR ELEVATORS - DAY

His hands full from check-in, Marcus looks around even more
lost and overwhelmed than before. Unable to find a friendly
face, he studies his triple A pass -

                    LARA (O.C.)
          HEY, HOLD THE ELEVATOR!

She stops the doors from closing to the chagrin of the posh
clientele already in it. Waits for Marcus to enter first.

INT. SWISH ELEVATOR - DAY

                    LARA
          8th floor thanks. What floor you
          need?

He can't find that information. Shamelessly looking over his
shoulder -

                    LARA (CONT'D)
          Same, cool.

She hits a button and shoots the Operator a smile, which he
returns with a disgruntled shake of the head.

                    LARA (CONT'D)
          You're a 'participant' too, huh?

Avoiding eye contact, Marcus nods.

                    LARA (CONT'D)
          Cool. Exciting, right. Kinda
          shitting myself too though.

Marcus tries to conceal a LAUGH. Her openness is refreshing
but, again, not much appreciated by the others around them.

INT. PLUSH HOTEL HALLWAY - DAY

Marcus swipes his keycard as Lara keeps going -

                    MARCUS
               (almost a WHISPER)
          Uh, bye.

- to the room next door -

                    LARA
          Hey, what's your name?
               (before he can answer)
          Lunch is in 45 minutes. You coming?

INT. LUXURIOUS HOTEL RESTAURANT - NIGHT

Marcus and Lara sit gawping at the immense dining hall
buzzing with activity.

                    LARA
          I'm making the most of this.

Marcus clocks One, TWO, Three and FOUR, eating and chatting
like best buddies.

When the food arrives it's more like tiny works of art. Lara
pokes hers with a fork -

                    LARA (CONT'D)
          Ew, what the hell is it!?

                    WAITER
          Our finest haute cuisine. A
          composition of seared goose breast
          and pheasant confit, bound in a
          panko crust, with sumptuously
          sauteed greens, hand-picked and
          locally harvested, complimented by
          truffle oil and orange foam.

                         LARA
               What?? Where's the rest of it?

                         WAITER
                    (humouring her)
               This is the first course. Of ten.

Lara GRUMBLES as she bravely lifts a forkful to her mouth.
Marcus waits for her to go first, watching expectantly for
her reaction.

EXT. FOOD TRUCK ON BUSTLING CITY STREET - NIGHT

WE FOLLOW as Marcus and LARA tuck into big juicy burgers -

                         LARA
               Oh my God, I've heard of you!
               You're, amazing! You got the
               highest score in Half-Life Hunter
               and Final Retribution. You could go
               pro tomorrow. Everyone thinks so.
                    (off Marcus's expression)
               You don't want to!?!

                         MARCUS
               Design is more me.

                         LARA
               But it pays nowhere near!

                         MARCUS
                    (shrugs)
               I'd prefer to be anonymous.

A ROUGH GUY barges into Marcus, knocking his burger to the
ground -

                         LARA
               Hey! Asshole!! Hey, you need to pay
               for that!

                         MARCUS
               It's okay.

The Rough Guy turns back -

                         GUY
               What? You talkin' to me!?

                         MARCUS
               No, don't worry about it. Sorry.

Marcus attempts to coax Lara away.

                         LARA
               What - Don't you say sorry!

The Guy continues on his way MUMBLING ANGRILY -

                    GUY
          I don't worry about nothin'.

Lara looks down. Marcus only had three bites at most.

                    LARA
          What a waste. Here.

She offers him the rest of her burger -

                    MARCUS
          Its okay.

                    LARA
          Take it. I'm used to sharing.
              (Marcus submits)
          And don't let people push you
          around like that.

INT. LAVISH HOTEL LOUNGE AREA - NIGHT

Lara PLONKS down next to Marcus - hands over a hotdog -

                    MARCUS
          Can we eat in here?

She opens a can of soda, shrugs. Can't see how its a problem.

                    LARA
          That your Mom calling?

                    MARCUS
          Dad. He worries.

                    LARA
          It's just you and him?

Marcus nods.

                    LARA (CONT'D)
          That's nice, right? Nobody will
          even notice I'm gone.
              (off Marcus's look)
          Three sisters, two brothers. Gonna
          be good to have a room to myself.
              (checks her watch)
          The press conference starts soon.
              (getting to her feet)
          Come, watch it in my room.

Again, Marcus relents.

INT. PRESS CONFERENCE (LARA'S HOTEL ROOM TV) - NIGHT

Resembling a Comic Con and White House press conference
rolled into one - A hip professional thirty-something
ANNOUNCER steps onto the stage.

> ANNOUNCER
> Thank you all for coming. Mr. Niko
> (over WHOOPS and CHEERS)
> Mr. Niko is going to give a short
> announcement before the Q&A segment
> and selection of players. So,
> without further ado, please welcome
> Mr. Tom Niko.

ROCK CONCERT MANIA ERUPTS as a rich, white, flashy douchebag
stands in front of the FLASHING cameras for a ridiculous
length of time before finally -

> TOM NIKO
> Thank you, thank you. I'll keep
> this brief so I don't give away too
> much before the spectacle of
> tomorrow night's events. I'd like
> to start by saying I was told by so
> many naysayers that releasing a
> horror game as a first for my new
> console was a mistake. But anybody
> that knows me knows I didn't get
> where I am without taking risks.
> (UPROARIOUS APPLAUSE)
> This is a scary game, but *I* trust
> *my* public can handle it. This is
> for real thrill-seekers only. And I
> guarantee it will be remembered in
> years to come as one of the best
> and scariest ever.
> (IRREPRESSIBLE APPLAUSE)
> On that monumental night in our
> remarkable stadium - a true sight
> to behold, I'm sure you'll agree.
> (the dime-sized device)
> 20 participants will be dropped
> into the game with randomly
> selected abilities. We will have 20
> substitute in case the game gets
> too much for some, which we are
> sure it will - Sorry in advance
> guys, you have been warned.

Everyone LAUGHS/CLAPS.

MARCUS swallows nervously.

                    TOM NIKO (CONT'D)
          What makes this game so scary is
          the AI's ability to adapt and
          create a completely tailored and
          unique experience.
                    (the audience laps it up)
          On the night, the game will run for
          around two hours and will be
          everything you expect from Kagami
          Games Inc, and then some.
                    (THUNDERING OVATION)
          Questions?

Motioning to the first correspondent -

                    CAUCASIAN FEMALE REPORTER
          How will players look within the
          game? Will they play specific
          characters?

                    TOM NIKO
          For this demonstration, they will
          look like themselves. However, when
          the game rolls out next month,
          players do not have to. This will
          add to the fun, and also help avoid
          in-game bullying or assaults on
          particular groups.

                    CAUCASIAN FEMALE REPORTER
          You're heralding a disguise mode on
          the game a good thing, but it's not
          solving the primary issue -

                    TOM NIKO
               (SCOFFS)
          - Is that a question? I agree with
          your statement, but even *I* can't
          fix that problem overnight.

The crowd still fully on Tom's side CHEER and CLAP with every
remark. He looks to -

                    OLD CAUCASIAN MALE REPORTER
          What kind of game is this? Maze?
          MMO? Running and gunning?

                    TOM NIKO
          Our demo tomorrow night will be a
          kind of last man standing mode.
          Makes for better television. But
          really its all of them rolled into
          one. It depends on how you want to
          play it.

                    ASIAN MALE REPORTER
          How much like the saleable game
          will the event be?
                    (MORE)

                    ASIAN MALE REPORTER (CONT'D)
          You say that a disguise mode has
          been disabled. What other parts of
          the game do you have external
          control of for it's unveiling?

                    TOM NIKO
          Only that. It will simply prevent
          confusion for the spectators. It
          also allows our gamers their
          fifteen minutes.

Lara is excited at the prospect, Marcus is petrified.

Tom looks toward another Reporter but -

                    ASIAN MALE REPORTER
                (LOUD and determined)
          What fail-safe measures are in
          place to prevent this new
          technology from hacking?

                    TOM NIKO
          Everything necessary -

                    ASIAN MALE REPORTER
          - What I'm getting at is there must
          be some form of transference of
          consciousness and so -

                    TOM NIKO
          - I cannot get into the secrets of
          the tech -

                    ASIAN MALE REPORTER
          - that means there's a real risk
          that mind hacking could become a
          thing.

Conspiratorial WHISPERS ripple around the room. Tom SHUFFLES
uncomfortably.

                    TOM NIKO
          I assure you the technology has
          been tested rigorously. It's
          perfectly safe.

Asian Male Reporter is cut off. Tom turns to -

                    YOUNG LATINO REPORTER
          Can you tell us more about the
          device? Is the player's
          consciousness transferred to the
          game? Or the game being played out
          in their mind?

Tom tries to hide his agitation and change the focus -

                    TOM NIKO
          I really cannot say. Like a
          magician, I don't want to give away
          my tricks, it could ruin the
          illusion for all involved. And
          neither do I want to give away my
          competitive edge.

MOST REPORTERS LAUGH.

                    BLACK MALE REPORTER
          If players are controlling
          themselves in the game as they
          would in real life, what's stopping
          them from acting out what they do?

                    TOM NIKO
          The device sends a signal to the
          part of the brain that controls
          motion. It is just like dreaming,
          the mind is active, the body is
          asleep.

Tom moves back to -

                    OLD CAUCASIAN MALE REPORTER
          Weren't you tempted to be a part of
          the game, being a self-professed
          gaming nerd yourself?

                    TOM NIKO
          I would if I could, but
          unfortunately I'm working tomorrow
          night.

                    CAUCASIAN FEMALE REPORTER
          How do players control the game
          without controls?

                    TOM NIKO
          Just like they would control their
          own actions in the real world,
          their minds. There is no longer
          anything between the game and the
          player. You can now completely
          escape into other worlds, without
          the need for clunky equipment.

                    BLACK MALE REPORTER
          Will it be safe to run on a
          domestic electricity supply? What
          would happen in a power -

Conveniently the Reporter's microphone goes off unexpectedly.

                    TOM NIKO
          I'm sorry, I didn't catch that.
          Looks like we're out of time.

Tom steps back from the podium, his smile strained as the CROWD ERUPTS INTO A FRENZY OF QUESTIONS.

INT. BACKSTAGE

Furious, Tom storms toward his punching bag/PA, NANCY -

                    TOM NIKO
          What the fuck was that!?

Trying hard to placate -

                    NANCY
          I assure you they weren't the
          questions they gave us.

Tom waves a finger in her face -

                    TOM NIKO
          I will not be blind-sided like that
          again, do you hear me!!

                    NANCY
          Loud and clear. I must say you
          handled it amaz -

Tom snatches a bottled water and storms off. Nancy SIGHS, the strain of the job almost too much.

INT. PRESS CONFERENCE on TV (LARA'S HOTEL ROOM)

APPLAUSE WANING until Tom steps back on stage, not a trace of the venom he showed backstage. Over the FRENZIED QUESTIONS -

                    TOM NIKO
          We have invited some of the best
          gamers with the highest scores on
          various online Kayami Games to play
          Alien Abduction. However, only half
          will be the first to play the most
          anticipated game of all time. The
          rest will be placed on standby. So
          its now time to select the very
          lucky players.

                    LARA
          Oh my God this is it! Good luck.
              (fingers crossed; Sotto)
          Please, please, please.

As Tom announces names, they appear on a list behind him.

Lara and Marcus listen with bated breath - one name almost sounds like Lara (Lola).

                    LARA (CONT'D)
          Damn!

Marcus SIGHS.

                    LARA (CONT'D)
              Don't give up hope yet.

                    TOM NIKO
          Now, the final participant -

Marcus and Lara exchange dejected looks.

                    TOM NIKO (CONT'D)
          - to play Alien Abduction: Endless
          Terror is - Marcus Gordon.

Stunned - sure he must have misheard - sure enough, his name
appears on the list. Lara SCREAMS, giddy with excitement,
pulls Marcus in for a bear hug.

                    TOM NIKO (CONT'D)
          Congratulations. I look forward to
          watching these talented gamers and
          our heroes of tomorrow night's
          event. Can we get a round of
          applause.

The crowd comply with zest.

Marcus is lost for words.

PLAYER BRIEFING/ORIENTATION MONTAGE - DAY

Next morning, a DESK CLERK checks Marcus and Lara's passes,
pointing them in opposite direction.

As he enters an OPULENT FUNCTION ROOM, Marcus is made to hand
over his phone.

During a talk Marcus spots One, Two, Three and Four chatting
familiarly again.

SUBSTITUTES are gathered around a large CONFERENCE ROOM. A
list shows Lara's name last - She hangs her head. A floor
plan of the Auditorium shows one substitute behind each
player. Lara regains a glimmer of hope.

Across a PALATIAL HALL Lara waves at Marcus as they proceed
to sign numerous lengthy non-disclosure agreements - no time
for reading.

Marcus looks up - gamers One, Two, Three and Four aren't
signing anything. Three reaches in his pocket, takes out his
phone. Two catches his eye, stops him.

A screen shows a close-up of the tiny device the SPEAKER on stage is holding. In the demonstration a TEST SUBJECT inserts the earpiece, TAPS it and slumps in the chair as if asleep.

PARTICIPANTS complete extensive medical questionnaires. Lara pauses on a Secondary Emergency Contact section. Marcus too.

On a slideshow, diagrams are shown with words like inhibit, radio waves, limbic system, activate, primary motor cortex.

Goody bags are doled out containing personalized rucksacks, T-shirts, beanies, you name it - all the usual tat.

Kid rummages intently. Nearby Two shows him a console voucher. Marcus finds one in his own bag - *how did she know?*

On their way out they are made to sign another disclosure agreement promising not to sell the merch. Marcus skims and spots mention of a $10,000 fine. Lara twists her face and points at her name. Gets a *what can you do* shrug in reply.

INT. HOTEL CAFE - DAY

Finally reunited, Marcus's face drops when he sees Lara's goody bag -

                    MARCUS
          20?

                    LARA
          Yeah.

                    MARCUS
          Substitute 20?

                    LARA
          Yeah, why?

The penny drops, Lara's smile fades -

                    LARA (CONT'D)
          Shit, you're *player* 20. I
          completely forgot.

Both feel genuine disappointment, and guilt.

                    GUIDE
          Tour bus leaves in 5!

Marcus and Lara just sat down! They pick up their stuff to eat on the move.

EXT. THE DOME - DAY

The Participants look up in awe at the massive structure in all it's imposing glory.

                    GUIDE
          Scan your Triple A passes to enter.
          Once inside, hand your phones over
          to security.

                    LARA
          Again!? We just got them back!

WE FOLLOW as they filter through and are led to -

INT. BACKSTAGE

Lara and Marcus bring up the rear. Those in front SCREAM.
One, Two, Three and Four hang back, CLAPPING coolly. It takes
a moment to discern what all the fuss is about -

                    LARA
          Oh my God, look!

Marcus's jaw drops. In the centre of the crowd is Tom Niko
with his trademark fixed grin -

                    TOM NIKO
          Thank you everyone, congratulations
          on being the chosen few to be a
          part of this historical event. I
          hope everyone is having fun so far.

WHOOPS, CLAPS and CHEERS. They hang on his every word,
something he's clearly used to -

                    TOM NIKO (CONT'D)
          This is going to be such an
          exciting night you'll remember for
          the rest of your lives. So, now
          that you're in the picture, I hope
          you can relax a little, and most of
          all - have fun!

APPLAUSE in all the right places. Clearly staged to make a
quick getaway, Nancy WHISPERS in Tom's ear.

                    TOM NIKO (CONT'D)
          Unfortunately I have to love you
          and leave you. See you tonight!

Tom gives a few high fives as he makes a swift exit
surrounded by his entourage. Nancy gives him a squirt of hand
sanitizer.

                    LARA
          Wow, Tom Niko in the flesh!
          Amazing.

Marcus is awestruck.

INT. HOTEL FUNCTION ROOM - NIGHT

The gamers are gathered together for a pre-launch buffet.
Marcus picks at his plate -

                    LARA
          Not hungry? What's up? Nervous?
               (Marcus nods)
          You're an amazing gamer, that's why
          you're here. Everyone wishes they
          were in your position. Me included!
          You'll be fine.

Marcus is not convinced.

                    LARA (CONT'D)
          You're a way better gamer than me
          and I wouldn't be worried. It's
          exciting!

                    MARCUS
          It's so - public.

                    LARA
          It's the chance of a lifetime. You
          can do it.

TENSE SILENCE.

                    MARCUS
          We could swap places.

Lara almost chokes on her food.

                    LARA
               (fighting temptation)
          No Marcus you can't. Thank you, but
          no. You'd regret it.

Marcus shrugs.

                    MARCUS
          But the media, audience, everyone
          online! You seem like you could
          handle it.

                    LARA
          Wow, that's more than I've heard
          you speak since we met.

Marcus smiles in spite of himself.

                    LARA (CONT'D)
          I couldn't take that away from you.
          You came all this way. And not by
          chance, by gaming skill! Forget
          what people might say. Plus, I'll
          be right behind. Literally!!

She SMILES supportively at him. He attempts to SMILES back.

                    LARA (CONT'D)
          You might even enjoy it. And win!
          Imagine!?

INT. THE DOME, BACKSTAGE - NIGHT

Last minute finishing touches are made around them. The
gamers are perfectly coordinated with the sleek surroundings
in numbered T-shirts. UNUSUALLY QUIET, even Lara is nervous.

                    LARA
          Gaming history. Think I need the
          bathroom. May just shit myself.

Marcus LAUGHS.

                    GUIDE/RUNNER
          It's time, so like the run-though
          earlier, get in order. Players on
          the right, substitutes left.

They SHUFFLE into place and wait. Listen. Nervously
contemplate. Lara glances at Marcus MUMBLING TO HIMSELF.
Others chat, breathe, limber up as if heading into battle.

                    MARCUS
          You can do this. For Mom.

Lara gives Marcus an encouraging thumbs up. Apprehensive, he
returns the gesture. A HUSH of anticipation. Eyes filled with
wonder as the lights fade -

                    ANNOUNCEMENT (O.C.)
          Friends, may we have you attention.
          Please welcome tonight's heroes.

                    GUIDE/RUNNER
          Just like we practiced. In 3, 2, -

THE CROWD ROARS. One confidently takes the lead. Each Gamer
NAMED AS THEY EMERGE. Marcus edges closer to the curtain,
visibly more debilitated by fear.

                    LARA (O.C.)
          Hey! Just watch the person in
          front. You can do this.

Momentarily distracted.

                    GUIDE/RUNNER
          Keep moving!

Marcus glances back one last time, no turning back now.

As he trails at the back of the line, Lara cheers hardest.

                    LARA
          He did it!

The Other Substitutes think she's nuts.

INT. THE DOME, AUDITORIUM

The CROWD ERUPTS WITH EXCITEMENT. Spared no expense, every
aspect of the design is immaculately thought out with the
idea firmly in mind that the world will be watching.

The energy is a combination of the Wall Street Stock Exchange
and the Superbowl.

- Sponsor ads fly across digital perimeter displays.

- A digital clock counts down to the launch on the huge
central scoreboard above.

- A Twitter feed moves around the spectator balconies.

INT. THE DOME, GAMERS CIRCLE

Onto a circular stage in the middle of the Auditorium, the
gamers take their seats in a smooth choreographed motion. The
world's media watching their every move - no spot unwatched.

Marcus takes in the extraordinary milieu as he sits. He
glances up, his face on the 50 foot screen. Like a deer in
headlights he clocks the camera. It stays on him until a
WHISTLE from the Guide/Runner breaks his gaze.

In front of each gamer is a large TV screen. The huge screen
behind the stage now shows the Substitutes take their seats.
Cutaways of spectators and other media. Marcus feels a hand
on his shoulder.

                    LARA
          We're actually doing it!

To their left -

                    ONE
          Sit down Sub.

Eyes roll -

                    LARA
          Whatever. Narc.

Marcus turns back to Lara and smiles, catches himself staring
and self-consciously looks down. Hands trembling. Scooting
forward -

                    LARA (CONT'D)
          Good thing you don't need a
          controller.

One shoots daggers. Lara gives as good as she gets.

Marcus looks at Nineteen/Kid to his right, wide-eyed with
excitement. One, nonchalant to the point of boredom at his
left. Like the opening of a rock concert, MUSIC BOOMS and
lights flash in time. The CROWD GOES WILD.

INT. THE DOME, STAGE

Tom enters to a standing ovation, DEAFENING WHOOPS AND CHEERS
from everyone, including media crews.

                    TOM NIKO
               (SHOUTING over the THRONG)
          Welcome everybody to my Temple of
          gaming. The Dome. I hope you are as
          excited as I am for the unveiling
          of my new game *and* game-changing
          technology.

Transfixed, Marcus looks up at his idol. Like everyone else,
hanging on his every word.

                    TOM NIKO (CONT'D)
          It's been a long time in the
          making. So enough from me, it's
          over to these stars.

The gamers are momentarily jarred as the circular stage
slowly begins to rotate. CHEERS CONTINUE TO EMANATE.

                    TOM NIKO (CONT'D)
          Gamers, friends, best of luck, and
          may the best player win!

Tom makes eye contact with One - they trade pally nods.
Marcus looks up to the clock counting down with only seconds
left. The audience COUNT DOWN -

- 00:00:00:10 -

Overwhelmed, Marcus tries to control his breathing.

- 00:00:00:09 -

Lara leans over and squeezes his shoulder.

- 00:00:00:08 -

The gamers place the device in their ears.

- 00:00:00:07 -

Press the device - it lights up.

- 00:00:00:06 -

Their eyes turn vague, bodies slump - Chairs automatically
adjust, holding them in position - upright.

INT. THE DOME'S CUSTOM BUILT GALLERY

- 00:00:00:05 -

The anticipation is palpable as PRODUCTION STAFF BEHIND THE
SCENES watch myriad screens.

- 00:00:00:04 -

INT. GAMERS CIRCLE

The screens come to life.

- 00:00:00:03 -

We see the POV of gamers begin to show.

- 00:00:00:02 -

INT. LEVEL 1 DARK CORRIDOR (INSIDE THE GAME)

00:00:00:01 - A FAR OFF ROAR OF APPLAUSE.

As if waking from a dream, Marcus opens his eyes - looks down
a futuristic corridor. He wears a futuristic space suit,
holds a futuristic gun.

Familiar faces around him (gamers One, Six, SEVEN and
Nineteen/Kid - numbers on their suits).

                    KID
          This is amazing!!

*VISION MIXER in the Gallery makes sure that makes it to the
big screen.*

                    SEVEN
          Where's everyone else?

                    ONE
          Could be anywhere.

                    SIX
          Uh, should we look for them?

Marcus is too shy to speak up. One on the other hand is
focused and proficient, almost like he's done this before -

                         ONE
               No. We'll come across them soon
               enough. Let's get going. People are
               watching.

Marcus gulps, he really didn't need reminding.

                         SIX
               Do we stick together, separate?

                    KID, SEVEN, EVEN MARCUS
               - STICK TOGETHER.

One takes the lead. Tentative, the rest follow.

INT. SCIENCE LAB (LEVEL 3)

DISARRAY - something went very wrong here. Kid TOUCHES
EVERYTHING he passes -

                         KID
               So real!

Acting grouchy because she's actually really scared -

                         SEVEN
               I don't like these flashing lights.
               Can hardly see a thing.

                         KID
               You scared? Guess what, that's the
               point.

INT. THE DOME, PRESENTATION PLATFORM

WE SEE Tom wears an earpiece as he turns back to the crowd -

                         TOM NIKO
               Some disorientation is to be
               expected. Remember, they're in a
               completely alien environment with
               real sensations they'd never
               experience in normal life.

INT. DIMLY LIT CORRIDOR

The gamers squint into the darkness, moving catlike, nerves
taut. Marcus and Six glance up at huge scratches on the
ceiling - eyes full of dread.

An INDECIPHERABLE yet unsettling DISTANT SOUND. In WHISPERS -

                         SIX
               You hear that?

Still too nervous to speak. Marcus nods -

                    KID
          Yep.

                    SEVEN
          Uh-huh - Damn automatic doors!
          Could be anything on the other
          side.

Ready to fire at anything that moves, they walk through,
keeping close, moving slow.

                    SIX
          You have played video games before,
          right?

                    KID
          My gun is heavy.

                    TOM NIKO (O.S.)
             (faint as if far away)
          - no menu screens or map views.
          It's all integrated -

They all heard that.

                    MARCUS
          I-i-it's Tom Niko.

INT. GAMERS CIRCLE

Back and forth from Tom to Marcus's screen, Lara absorbs it
all. On Marcus's screen, direct to camera -

                    ONE
          - the real world. Ignore it.

                    MARCUS (O.S.)
          How do you know?

                    ONE
             (taken aback)
          I heard it too.

Lara watches the next bulkhead open as she leans forward.

INT. PITCH BLACK SECTION OF CORRIDOR

One uses a light on his gun. The others eventually find
theirs too.

                    LARA (O.S.)
          Marcus?

Marcus's leaps in shock and suddenly all guns point at him.

                    MARCUS
          Lara?

Everyone looks around, confused.

                    LARA (O.S.)
          Cool.

                    MARCUS
          Weird!

                    ONE
          What's wrong with you?

Kid is bewildered, Six and Seven are just annoyed.

                    MARCUS
          M-my - friend.
               (realizes he sounds crazy)
          Never mind.

The others have already moved on -

                    LARA (O.S.)
          I see everything. I can give you
          pointers.

                    KID
          That's cheating.

                    MARCUS
          You hear her too!?

                    ONE
               (belligerent)
          I think your device is
          malfunctioning. Maybe exit the game
          and get it sorted.

INT. GAMERS CIRCLE

Lara SPEAKS in his right ear (nearest Kid).

                    LARA
          Just say if you need me.

Lara glances round as she leans back - nobody has noticed.

INT. MAINTENANCE ROOM (LEVEL 1)

Alone, Thirteen checks out everything he lays eyes on: duct
tape, a drill -

                    THIRTEEN
          Huh, works.

Light sticks and a welding torch in a dusty box - also work.
He wipes his dusty hands on his spacesuit. Astonished by the
detail.

SOMETHING OUTSIDE!

He readies his gun as he creeps to the door, hesitant to open
it. The SOUND COMES CLOSER. He's not prepared when it opens -
SCREAMS, GUNSHOTS.

A BLOOD-CURDLING SCREAM - from Thirteen. NINE rushes over.

                    NINE
          Shit, sorry, I thought you were one
          of those things.

                    THIRTEEN
          Shit, this fucking kills man!

                    NINE
          What should I do?

                    THIRTEEN
          Fuck this! EXIT GAME.

Thirteen vanishes into thin air.

                    NINE
          Whoa!!

INT. GAMERS CIRCLE

Sweating, Thirteen comes to as if from a night terror. Finds
all eyes and cameras on him.

                    SUBSTITUTE 13
                (excited)
          Does this mean it's my turn?

Rushing over -

                    RUNNER
          It's been five minutes. You're the
          first to exit, you definitely done?

                    THIRTEEN
          It hurt so bad!

He checks his leg - not a mark. Touches it - perfectly fine.

                    RUNNER
          You need to find a medikit,
          remember. Just like any other game.
          You ready?

He nods and presses his earpiece - slumps.

                    SUBSTITUTE 13
          What the -

INT. CORRIDOR FROM MAINTENANCE ROOM

Nine tiptoes away when - A SCREAM. He spins round firing
indiscriminately again in pure panic.

                    THIRTEEN
          Help!

Nine dashes back, surprised to see Thirteen has reappeared.

                    THIRTEEN (CONT'D)
          Get me a medikit!

                    NINE
          A what?

                    THIRTEEN
          A MEDIKIT! There has to be one
          somewhere nearby.

                    NINE
              (recalls)
          I think I've seen one!

Nine DARTS OFF -

                    THIRTEEN
          Wait! Don't leave me.

                    NINE
          But - Can you walk?

Looking at his leg - unlikely. MOANS OF AGONY as Nine tries
to help Thirteen to his feet - puts him back down.

                    THIRTEEN
          How does it hurt so bad? I know its
          just in my head.

                    NINE
          Wait here. Keep quiet.

                    THIRTEEN
          Keep quiet!? Why?

Nine is gone. Thirteen alone again. Glancing down at his
bloodstained suit he catches sight of his number -

                    THIRTEEN (CONT'D)
          Might've known.

INT. ENGINE ROOM 1 (LEVEL 1)

Gamers EIGHT, ELEVEN, FIFTEEN, and SIXTEEN follow behind
Three and Four.

                    ELEVEN
          I'm Jamie.

                    FIFTEEN
          Ryan.

With the same authoritative air as One -

                    THREE
          This isn't Animal Crossing.

INT. SLEEPING QUARTERS (LEVEL 2)

One, closely followed by the others, enters to discover the
aftermath of more past carnage. Marcus touches blood on a
sleep pod door -

                    MARCUS
          Warm!

                    ONE
          Be ready.

Seven stiffens. Sweeps her beam all around.

                    KID
          For what?

                    SIX
          Anything.

An unsettling WHIR - all brandish their weapons at Kid having
pressed a button.

                    SEVEN
          Cut it out Kid! It's all very real,
          we get it.

                    SIX
          Are you trying to get shot?

Kid sheepishly steps back from the pod. They move on. Seven
smiles back sarcastically.

A flash of movement behind them! Marcus spins round, sees
nothing. A SQUELCH -

                    SEVEN
          That better not be you again Kid!

They hear another SQUELCH. Try to pinpoint it's whereabouts.

                    ONE
          Shh!

                    KID
          Hello?

                    EVERYONE
          Shhh!

Suddenly something appears, but before anyone else can
register it, One FIRES and it goes down. Wide eyed, they
check it out.

                    KID
          What the hell is that?

It looks vaguely like a creepy child.

                    ONE
          Someone here doesn't like kids.

Kid studies everyone's face. Seven looks freaked -

                    KID
          Boo!

Seven falls back with a CLATTER onto an instrument panel on
the wall. It lights up.

                    SEVEN
          Idiot!

It's strangely familiar to Marcus, he types in a code - a MAP
appears.

                    SIX
          How did you know to do that?

                    MARCUS
          I, don't know, I just -

                    ONE
          Looks like you're a Navigator.

                    KID
          Cool. I hope I'm the Captain.

Marcus zooms in on the 3D map. One large area flashes red.

                    SEVEN
          I hope you're not.

                    KID
          You should be the Janitor -

                    ONE
          The Cargo Hold. Directly below.
          Come on.

                         SEVEN
              But its flashing red!

                          ONE
              Yeah, that's where the action is.
              It's what we're here for.

                          KID
              Cool!

All other faces are full of uncertainty.

INT. MAINTENANCE ROOM

Lying motionless in a pool of blood Thirteen YELPS as the
door WHOOSHES open. Nine tosses a Medikit to him, hitting -

                       THIRTEEN
              Ah, my leg! Asshole!

                          NINE
              Sorry.

                       THIRTEEN
              What do I do with it?

It doesn't open. Nine takes a look.

                          NINE
              Dunno.

There's a single button. Nine presses it.

                       THIRTEEN
              Is it doing anything?

Nine shakes his head. Spotting the health bar light up -

                   THIRTEEN (CONT'D)
              Wait, stop!

Snatching it back, Thirteen presses the button repeatedly,
realizes the bar only appears when the button is held down -

                   THIRTEEN (CONT'D)
              It's working!

The pain across Thirteen's face fades and the injury heals
before their eyes and is almost completely healed.

                          NINE
              That was bad-ass.

Getting to his feet. A SLIGHT LIMP -

                       THIRTEEN
              Next time you can get shot.

INT. GAMERS CIRCLE

Lara leans forward again -

                    LARA
          Marcus, look for medikits.

INT. DARK STAIRWELL DOWN TO LEVEL 1

At the back of the group Marcus GASPS in shock. Everyone
freezes and turns to him -

                    MARCUS
             (to those around him)
          Sorry.

                    LARA (O.S.)
          They're square and orange -

INT. GAMERS CIRCLE

                    LARA
          - and the injured has to hold down
          the button.

A Runner looks over, somewhat suspicious. Lara shiftily leans
back and shoots a condescending smile.

INT. DARK STAIRWELL

They continue their decent tentatively.

                    MARCUS
             (WHISPERS)
          Thank you.

As if speaking to God -

                    KID
          Thank you.

                    MARCUS
          Shh!

Disgruntled, One stops and looks back.

INT. GAMERS CIRCLE

Lara, still being watched, cups a hand over her mouth -

                    LARA
          Don't mention it.

INT. MAINTENANCE CORRIDOR

Armed and ready, Nine and Thirteen disappear round a bend.

                    THIRTEEN
          You must have used some of my
          health before.

                    NINE
          I didn't. I feel exactly the same.

                    THIRTEEN
          There was nothing wrong with you
          was there, but I'm still not 100%.

He limps as they arrive at a -

INT. LARGE FREIGHT ELEVATOR

Stacked high with boxes - the contents of some spilled.

                    THIRTEEN (O.S.)
          I can't hear anything.

DING! The doors open.

                    NINE
          Wait! No!

Nine ducks out of the way leaving Thirteen standing puzzled.

All is QUIET. Nine gets back up, but encourages Thirteen to
step inside first before cautiously following.

Thirteen hits a button at random. The doors close. Nothing is
happening. He PUNCHES the button repeatedly. Nine grabs his
arm.

They hear a definite GROAN. The fear on their faces
multiplies as they turn to one another. Thirteen pushes a box
aside, sees the back of -

                    THIRTEEN
               (Whispers)
          A man!

Nine covers Thirteen's mouth and pulls him away. They huddle
in terror. Nine frantically pushes buttons to open the doors
again. They CREAK open and closed again as if jammed. The Man
slowly turns, the movements jerky - something's not quite
right. Mouth agape, horrifying - like having never seen one
before, a man were created from a really bad description -
THEY SHRIEK.

INT. THE DOME, TIERED SEATS

Perceptions of the situation is very different between
participants and audience. The AUDIENCE LAUGH at the display
of fear on screen as if it were a three stooges skit.

INT. FREIGHT ELEVATOR

The Grotesque Man LUNGES, Thirteen falls back and out -

INT. MAINTENANCE CORRIDOR BY FREIGHT ELEVATOR

The Grotesque Man salivates on Thirteen - he SCREAMS.

                    THIRTEEN
          Get him off!!

Panic-stricken Nine fumbles for his gun -

                    THIRTEEN (CONT'D)
               (diving for cover)
          But don't shoot me again!

BOOM! It's head EXPLODES and body falls to the ground.
Thirteen covered in a bloody mess.

                    THIRTEEN (CONT'D)
          This is disgusting.
               (catching his breath)
          At least now we know what we're up
          against.

Nine shakes his head - Thirteen doesn't know the half of it.

                    THIRTEEN (CONT'D)
          Huh?

INT. LONG CORRIDOR TO CARGO HOLD

Almost complete darkness. This is the red area on the map -
ALARMS SOUND, lights flicker. One takes the lead like a real
commando. Suddenly, over the RACKET - GUNFIRE and SCREAMS.

                    KID
          More gamers!

One marches ahead straight towards what a normal person would
run from. Seven hangs back, pushes Kid in front.

INT. CARGO HOLD (LEVEL 1)

The main door slides open to reveal PANDEMONIUM. One's face
lights up -

                    ONE
          Now that's what I'm talking about.

Numerous gamers battle a HORDE OF GROTESQUE PEOPLE like the
man in the elevator (we'll call them Weirdos).

Without hesitation One gets right in the thick of it, FIRING
into the horde. The rest of the group remain in a huddle,
unable to believe their eyes.

Marcus watches One, Two and Three holding their own well.

                    LARA (O.S.)
          You can do it!

Marcus summons the courage and breaks from the group - Not
one to be outdone, Kid follows suite and BLINDLY OPENS FIRE.

As Two Weirdos advance toward them, Seven bolts out, pressing
the door shut behind her.

Six's heroic SHOT misses, attracting more unwanted attention.
Marcus quickly finishes them off. Rushing forward -

                    KID
          A medikit!

Marcus provides cover fire in the nick of time.

INT. LONG CORRIDOR FROM CARGO HOLD

Seven sprints as far away as possible.

INT. CARGO HOLD

Amid the CARNAGE, on the move Marcus FIRES to keep Weirdos at
bay. His eyes search, scrutinize and determine the most
immediate threats - he may even be starting to enjoy himself.

Cornered, Eleven FIRES indiscriminately until CLICK-CLICK-
CLICK - Three Weirdos close in -

                    ELEVEN
          EXIT GAME!

The Weirdos fall in a pile where she stood, leaving Marcus
and Kid stunned.

Fifteen battles a Weirdo but another approaches from behind.
Marcus winces as they overwhelm her. Once painfully finished
off, Fifteen disappears from the game just like Eleven.
Having witnessed this horror -

                    SIX
          I'm not sure this game is really
          for me.

Within earshot -

                    ONE
          Are you crazy!? It's better than
          reality.

Not something anyone could do in real life. One leaps and
flips in the air with ease as he fires on the move.
Mesmerized -

                    SIX
          Hey, how do you do that?

INT. PRESENTATION PLATFORM

                    TOM NIKO
               (Relief more than joy)
          Looks like some are getting used to
          it already. Now it's really getting
          started.
               (sotto)
          At last.

At the side of the stage Nancy is even more relieved.

INT. CARGO HOLD

Three shoots with absolute precision - every bullet hits a
Weirdo - checking his watch between shots, his score goes up
and up.

Suddenly a NEWBIE appears, completely disoriented -

                    KID
          Who are you?

The Newbie (Substitute 11) has no time to respond before
being instantly and agonizingly killed by the Weirdo's that
had piled on his predecessor.

Whilst EIGHTEEN picks off Weirdos with ease, she and Three
fire at the same one - it goes down. Each look at their
watches - Eighteen picked up the points.

Pissed, Three watches Eighteen run across the Cargo Hold
shooting successfully at others. Without warning Three shoots
her in the back - she disappears from the game.

INT. GAMERS CIRCLE

Eighteen wakes SCREAMING IN AGONY. Feels her back, taking a
moment to realize she is now fine -

                    EIGHTEEN
          One of the other gamers shot me!

She looks around for the culprit. A Runner hurries over to
calm her.

INT. PRESENTATION PLATFORM

Tom watches the COMMOTION below, listening to -

                    VOICE FROM EARPIECE/NINA (O.S.)
          It's as real as reality to the
          brain - That's the point. Don't
          worry, it's exactly what they asked
          for.

Concealing his mouth to speak into a clip mic.

INT. GALLERY

Amongst a room full of busy Production Staff, all with
numerous screens in front of them is Lead Programmer (NINA).
These are the people *really* running the show. In her ear -

                    TOM NIKO (O.S)
          Can't we dial it down?

Despite having no patience with Tom she is perfectly
diplomatic. A true pro -

                    NINA
          Its just started! Its going to get
          a whole lot worse too, but for a
          horror game that's a good thing.

She rolls her eyes. Those nearby shake their heads.

INT. PRESENTATION PLATFORM

Tom LAUGHS NERVOUSLY as Eighteen is escorted away RANTING AND
RAVING -

                    TOM NIKO
               (to the spectators)
          Gamers, a passionate bunch. That's
          what I love about them.

INT. GAMERS CIRCLE

Enthralled, Lara watches both the RUCKUS nearby and the 50
foot screen. She leans forward and just like Tom, she covers
her mouth -

                    LARA
          Marcus -

INT. CARGO HOLD

Definitely getting the hang of it, Marcus holds his own with
impeccable focus.

                    LARA (O.S.)
          - watch out for Three, he shot
          player Eighteen. Not an accident.

Just then the remaining Weirdos stand still - OSCILLATE.

                    SIX
          What are they doing?

Nearby -

                    SEVENTEEN
          Is it a glitch?

INT. CARGO HOLD

The Weirdos EXPLODE and reform into huge disturbing SPIDER-
LIKE CREATURES. Again, skewed as if imagined by someone who
has only heard a terrifying description - ghastly-looking and
completely unpredictable. Marcus notices One toss aside a
medikit and stand up, calmly taking aim, indicating -

                    MARCUS
          Its part of the game.

Seventeen is stabbed through the chest by a Spider, with her
last ounce of strength -

                    SEVENTEEN
          EXIT GAME!!

SEVENTEEN disappears and SUBSTITUTE 17 - arrives in the exact
same spot, just inches from the same fate.

INT. GALLERY

Watching on the bank of monitors -

                    NINA
          Spiders, every time. Lets see if
          anyone here has any new fears.

INT. CARGO HOLD

Three is surrounded and struggling -

                    THREE
          Theo!

One reacts - piquing Marcus's suspicions.

                    MARCUS
              (sotto)
         Theo?

Two Spiders attack Eight who yanks at a grenade ring and
holds on - taking out the Spiders and himself. Three is also
engulfed in the BLAST and One is flung across the room.

INT. GAMERS CIRCLE

Eight wakes HYPERVENTILATING, jarring nearby Spectators.

Three comes to in his chair without any confusion or
disorientation like the others -

                    THREE
         FUCK!! Are you kidding me!?

Obliged to now sit and watch, he angrily rips the device from
his ear. From across the rotating stage -

                    EIGHTEEN (O.S.)
         Woo! Haha. Karma Bitch!

Three turns to see Eighteen SARCASTICALLY SLOW CLAPPING and
giving him the finger. He eyes her with disdain and turns
away as Staff rushes to SILENCE her again.

INT. GALLERY

Staff CLICK AWAY on various devices -

                    NINA
         We need to alter the positioning of
         substitutes. They aren't lasting
         five seconds.

- with increased ferocity.

INT. GAMERS CIRCLE

SUBSTITUTE 8 complains whilst Eight is in full-blown panic
attack mode with a Medic by his side -

                    SUBSTITUTE 8
         Technically he exited the game so I
         should go in.

                    RUNNER
         That's not how it works.

                    SUBSTITUTE 8
         He chickened out. Everyone saw -

                    RUNNER
          - Sorry, it can't be done. If a
          gamer is killed they can't be
          substituted.

Lunging at Eight -

                    SUBSTITUTE 8
          You little bitch! Why didn't you
          Exit the Game!! You ruined my -

Cameras turn towards the action. Security rush in to block
any view of the fight.

INT. CARGO HOLD

Marcus FIRES at a Weirdo/Spider. Out of ammo and other
options he dives into a complex machine's workings. Suddenly
the Creature bursts into a CENTIPEDE-THING allowing it to
follow and quickly gain on him.

As Marcus scrambles out the other side he is dragged back -

                    SIX (O.S)
          The button!

Marcus sees Six concealed amongst complex equipment, looks
where Six POINTS. Hits the button - yanking his leg back just
before the Centipede is crushed. Six quickly pulls Marcus to
safety.

                    MARCUS
          Thank you. Ammo?

                    SIX
          I'm low. Seen plenty, just can't
          get to it.

He waves Marcus to follow onto a vehicle.

Marcus notices One across the Cargo Hold - listening to
someone remotely -

                    NINA (O.S.)
          - change objective. This chaos is
          starting to work against us.

                    ONE
          Yeah, it's definitely too much for
          most of them.

He REPEATEDLY FIRES at a Spider that eventually EXPLODES, but
reform into a FURRY SLITHERING CREATURE. It takes another
HAIL OF BULLETS before it is finally taken down.

                    SIX
          We don't have the firepower to kill
          'em all. We gotta get outta this
          place.

They scan round for an exit.

A running Weirdo EXPLODES into a WARPED WOLF-LIKE THING to
the horror of -

                    FOURTEEN
          EXIT GAME!

His sub appears momentarily. Survives longer than the rest by
instantly making a run for it.

Marcus spots Kid, cornered - grabs Six's gun and takes out
the Wolf with the last three rounds. Kid spins, wondering who
helped -

                    SIX
          Up here Kid!

He looks up but so do two nearby Creatures. Kid clambers over
the dead Wolf and onto the vehicle. A Spider gaining, Kid
throws something up - Ammo! Marcus and Six reload and take
out the two Creatures.

Two and Four provide SUPPRESSIVE FIRE to One, who escapes out
the main doors.

Momentarily, giving others - both gamers and Creatures - the
opportunity to do the same, fleeing in a all directions.

INT. GAMERS CIRCLE

Numerous gamers are back, breathing SIGHS OF RELIEF.

INT. GALLERY

                    TOM NIKO (O.S.)
          There's more out of the game than
          in. It's only been 20 minutes!

                    NINA
          It's challenging and scary, just
          like everyone expected. There are
          still about half the subs to go
          yet. And as long as we have a
          couple of our people in there we're
          golden.

With a clear undertone of contempt -

                    TOM NIKO (O.S.)
          Maybe *you* simply shouldn't have
          made it quite so difficult.

                    NINA
               (trying not to lose it)
          Make it too easy and nobody will be
          willing to spend $3k on *your* new
          console.
               (distracted)
          A snake-spider combo, that's new.
          Creepy.

INT. PRESENTATION PLATFORM

Tom watches SUBSTITUTE 12 plug in - SLUMP - the TV come to
life. The SNAKE/SPIDER MONSTROSITY attacks. The screen goes
black again and the Substitute returns as if from a
nightmare, CRYING WITH RELIEF, comforted by his forerunner.

                    TOM NIKO
          It's my reputation on the line!

Hoping not to be noticed Nancy timidly hands Tom prompt
cards. He snatches them angrily.

                    NINA (O.S.)
               (strained politeness)
          Yes I understand, it's *ours* too. So
          far public opinion is all good. Use
          the cards to get attention back to
          the game, or you. The new creatures
          are the perfect segue to explaining
          more about *your* new AI tech.

MONTAGE - VARIOUS

A) INT. LONG CORRIDOR - Numerous gamers flee. Nine reaches a
door - it won't open - tries the next one as a WOLF bounds
toward him - won't open either.

                    NINE
          EXIT GAME!

B) INT. GALLERY - Something is wrong with the screens.
Everyone sits and stares, dumbfounded.

C) INT. FREIGHT ELEVATOR - SUB FOURTEEN skids inside, hitting
buttons - a SPIDER/WEIRDO barrels closer to her. The buttons
light up - nothing happens. The Creature crashes into the
elevator as the doors close. Sub Fourteen miraculously
scrambles out unscathed.

D) INT. CARGO HOLD - The coast is clear(ish), Marcus, Six and
Kid make a run for another door. Kid trails, Marcus pulls him
along.

E) INT. NARROW CORRIDOR - Still being chased -

                    NINE (CONT'D)
          EXIT GAME!!

Still nothing happens.

F) INT. THE DOME, SPECTATOR LEVEL - Someone points to a
screen showing Nine clearly SHOUTING 'EXIT GAME', as the Wolf
furiously gains on him.

G) INT. VENT - Sub Fourteen rips a vent cover from the wall -
clambers in, but is yanked out SCREAMING.

INT. WEAPONS STORE

Filling up on ammo - COMMOTION from The Dome seeps through -

                    ONE
          What's going on out there?
               (no response)
          Hello?

STILL NO ANSWER.

As he clips one magazine after another to his belt, the
previous one disappears. His watch BEEPS: 'storage full'. He
picks up a couple more guns and coolly OPENS FIRE as he
vanishes out the door.

INT. NARROW CORRIDOR

Athletic-looking TEN strains to run, much slower than he
looks physically capable of as a a SNAKE-LIKE WEIRDO (no arms
or legs) wriggles after him at alarming speed.

                    TEN
          EXIT GAME!
               (continues running)
          EXIT GAME!!

It BURSTS into a Spider, leaps and rides him to the ground -
BLOODCURDLING SCREAMS -

INT. GAMERS CIRCLE

Ten is non-responsive in his chair. The screen in front of
him BLACK. SUBSTITUTE 10 shakes him, checks his breathing,
pulse. PANIC!

                    SUBSTITUTE 10
          MEDIC!

INT. SPECTATOR LEVEL

People hang over the balcony to get a better view as a Medic
uses a defibrillator on Ten.

INT. CURVED CORRIDOR

One stops, listens. The AGONISING SCREAMS continue to ECHO.
It's hard to know where exactly it's coming from (the game or
the Dome).

INT. GALLERY

Everyone exchanges looks of confusion as complex code moves
across their computer screens. SLAMMING down her headset -

                    NINA
          Can someone tell me what the hell
          is going on!? How can we be locked
          out!? This is no code I've seen
          before.

Her keyboard actions have no effect.

                    NINA (CONT'D)
          Where's it come from? This system
          is hack-proof.

Shrugs all round. Everyone turns to everyone else for
answers. Nina rushes to a bank of monitors -

                    NINA (CONT'D)
               (relieved)
          They're still playing.
               (to Vision Mixer)
          Just keep doing your thing.
          Hopefully we can fix this before
          anyone out there notices.

INT. GAMERS CIRCLE

Those in the vicinity of Nine SCREAM and turn away as he
violently convulses. His screen shows him being pulled limb
from limb by various monstrous creatures. His movements in
the seat mirror what we see on screen. His limbs bend and
CRACK in unnatural ways. Suddenly the screen is black - the
convulsions stop.

INT. PITCH DARK ROOM / COMMON ROOM (LEVEL 2)

Six rushes in first, followed by Thirteen, then Marcus and
Kid. The lights flicker to life.

                    SIX
          Where'd you come from?

Marcus picks up a Medikit. Miraculously nobody needs it.

                    THIRTEEN
          Never mind that, I need ammo.

                    KID
          Here.

He shares his out. As he unclips one, another appears in it's
place.

                    THIRTEEN
          Cool, at least you're good for
          something. Noticed you can't run
          for shit.

                    KID
          I'd beat you all in real life.

                    THIRTEEN
          Keep telling yourself that Kid.

                    KID
          Well then, no more favours. I might
          be slow, but I plan to win.

INT. GAMERS LEVEL

The rotating stage stops.

The atmosphere of the auditorium has switched to genuine
distress as the few Medics available are inundated with
commands.

Spectators look away from the main stage and down onto the
Gamers' Circle with increasing unease.

Lara watches the horror unfold nearby - Nine and Ten rushed
away on stretchers under black covers as more DISTRESSED
SHOUTS ERUPT.

Looking back at the stage - deserted.

INT. SMALL MAINTENANCE TUNNEL

One finds Nine lying in a bloody pool.

                    ONE
          Hey guys, this is weird.
               (turns Nine over)
          Nine is dead but didn't disappear
          from the game. Did someone change
          something? And if so, when?
                    (MORE)

                    ONE (CONT'D)
                 (off RADIO SILENCE)
             Hello, Hello?

He takes the magazine out of Nine's gun. Swaps guns when he
notices Nine's is actually a little better.

INT. GALLERY

Staff check cable connections and hit equipment.

                    ONE (O.S.)
             Can anyone hear me?

Suddenly FLOOR MANAGER BURSTS in -

                    FLOOR MANAGER
             This is a disaster. Tom's
             disappeared.

                    NINA
             He what! Why? Go find him.

Looking to the main viewing monitor -

                    NINA (CONT'D)
                 (off Floor Manager's
                  pacing)
             What?

Unable to find the words. The TV screens behind her show the
gamers' POVs. Many being attacked by Strange Creatures.

          NINA (CONT'D)   VISION MIXER
     We have audio and visual
     coming through. Those in the
     game haven't noticed any   Well actually --
     problem. Nobody out there
     could have either. Hey, are
     you listening?

                    FLOOR MANAGER
             Three gamers are dead.

                    NINA
                 (baffled)
             Uh, more than that. They're
             dropping like flies but it's fine -

                    FLOOR MANAGER
             - Not the game. Out there.
                 (off Nina's bemused look)
             In their seats!
                 (lets it sink in)
             In front of a stadium of people!

It takes a moment to register what she's saying.

                         NINA
             Is Nine one of 'em?

Floor Manager nods, wondering *What's your point.*

                         NINA (CONT'D)
             Just minutes ago?

                         FLOOR MANAGER
             Yes!

Nina takes over from the Vision Mixer to find the footage.
Replays One's POV -

                         NINA
             That's why.
                  (finding Nine dead)
             He's still in the game.

INT. PREP ROOM (LEVEL 3)

The room is so far untouched. Thirteen enters first.

                         THIRTEEN
             There's nothing in here.

                         SIX
             Exactly. Good.

          THIRTEEN   SIX
Its all clear out there [the   What?
corridor], for now anyway. We   (distracted)
need to keep moving.   I can't focus because of -

Six gestures to his head, hearing the PANIC AND CONFUSION in
the real world too -

                         THIRTEEN
             Nothing can be done about that.

The only one still focused on the game is Marcus, he gives
the room a quick once over -

                         KID
             What you looking for?

                         MARCUS
             Supplies.

                         SIX
             Just gimme a minute to adjust then.

          NINETEEN   THIRTEEN
-- Shhh! What did they --   Are they saying someone
                                   died!?

Even Marcus stops, listening intently.

                    SIX   NINETEEN
          Sounded like that.   Yeah, but who?

                         MARCUS
               Lara. Lara?

                         THIRTEEN
               Who or what is Lara?

                         MARCUS
               My, substitute.

                         THIRTEEN
               Huh?

                         KID
               She still not answering?

                         SIX
               Something's really wrong then.

                         THIRTEEN
               You're in on this crap too?

                         SIX
                    (Sarcastic)
               You'll just have to get used to it.

                         MARCUS
                    (to everyone)
               Should we exit?

                         KID
               No way, there's only one way I'm
               leaving. You do it if you want.

                         SIX
               It sounds serious out there Kid. If
               something is wrong, we're sitting
               ducks.
                    (stony resolve)
               EXIT GAME!

Six and Marcus lock eyes - all at once jolted by VIOLENT
BANGS AND SCRATCHES that dint the door.

INT. PASSAGEWAY TO PREP ROOMS

A Spider and Wolf hunt for a way in.

INT. GAMERS CIRCLE

Anxiety and fear spread like a Mexican wave through the
entire stadium when suddenly an ALARM SOUNDS.

                    ANNOUNCEMENT (OVERHEAD)
          Attention. Please calmly exit the
          building.

Confused faces, even from Security who jump into action
accordingly.

INT. PREP ROOM

                    MARCUS
               (reeling)
          EXIT GAME!

Nothing happens still.

          THIRTEEN   SIX
What the --   EXIT GAME!

                    SIX
          Are we not doing it right!?

Thirteen urges Kid to try -

                    KID
          I'm not doing it.

                    SIX
          Are you kidding!? You heard the
          announcement.

                    THIRTEEN
          If it's a false alarm they gotta
          let us back in. EXIT GAME!

Dismay set in -

                    ALL (EXCEPT KID)
          EXIT GAME!!

All still present - Stuck! Even Kid is distressed.

INT. PASSAGEWAY TO PREP ROOMS

The Spider and Wolf combine forming something way more
terrifying - It PUMMELS the door and wall with double the
violence.

INT. PREP ROOM

The door BUCKLES AND SPLITS from the CONSTANT BLOWS on the
other side - it can't hold much longer.

INT. CORRIDOR TO GALLERY

Baffled, Nina comes out. The ANNOUNCEMENT RUNNING ON A LOOP.

                    SECURITY (O.S.)
          This way please.

                    NINA
              (pulls free)
          Who the hell says so?

Nancy breathlessly battles against the reluctantly exiting
crowd. Indicating the broadcast -

                    NANCY
          Tom made me do it.

Off Nina's infuriated expression -

INT. GAMERS CIRCLE

ANARCHY - Substitutes and Surviving Gamers are herded out.
When urged toward the nearest exit with everyone, Lara is
reluctant -

                    LARA
          Where are we going?

                    FRIENDLY SECURITY GUARD
          Its an evacuation.

                    LARA
          But my friend, I need to help him.

Turning back to Marcus unconscious in his chair -

                    FRIENDLY SECURITY GUARD
          Him?
              (off Lara's nod)
          Sorry, right now, nobody can.

INT. THE DOME, CORRIDORS

The Friendly Security Guard and Lara join the THRONG -

                    LARA
          What do you mean?

He's already said too much.

                    LARA (CONT'D)
          Are the other gamers going to be
          okay?

                    SECURITY
          I can't say.

But his face says it all.

INT. OBSERVATION ROOM (LEVEL 2)

Marcus, Six and Kid help pull the injured Thirteen in. Marcus
hands him a Medikit - He knows what to do with it now.

                    THIRTEEN
               (pure rapture)
          Ahhh! How come nobody else has been
          hurt and I have twice.

                    SIX
          How are people doing for supplies?

                    KID
          Low.

Marcus stares in awe at the view of alien stars and planets.

                    MARCUS
               (lost in reverie)
          Same.

                    THIRTEEN
          Nothing.

Thirteen paces, no more limp. Slaps Marcus on the back -

                    THIRTEEN (CONT'D)
          Thank you friend.
               (at the view)
          Wow!

They each are enraptured -

                    KID
          You think we can go out there?

                    THIRTEEN
          The game's not impossible enough
          already!? One thing at a time Kid.

                    SIX
          If we can't reload we need another
          plan. How many medikits we got?

They check their watches.

                    KID
          One.

Grim-faced, Marcus and Thirteen shake their heads.

                    SIX
          Any ideas?

                    MARCUS
               (deep in thought)
          Maybe.

INT. PERSONNEL LOCKER

All is QUIET. Tentative, Seven finally plucks up the nerve to
climb out.

INT. PERSONNEL LOCKER ROOM (LEVEL 2)

Deserted - Seven's gun CLATTERS against the locker door - She
cringes. The door WHOOSHES open to her distress -

INT. DARK CORRIDOR

The stillness is unsettling. Eerie. Seven looks left, then
right. An eight legged figure SILENTLY SCUTTLES past the end
of the corridor unseen by her (its Marcus *et al*). She chooses
that way!

INT. WEAPONS STORE (LEVEL 2)

A FUSS GROWS outside -

                    MARCUS (O.S.)
          Guys, here it is!

                    THIRTEEN (O.S.)
          Yes! We so lucked out!

They tumble in, but their elation switches to disbelief.

The room is completely empty.

                    KID
          Where is it all?

STUNNED SILENCE. Too silent in fact -

                    SIX
          Um, do you hear anything, at all?

Only just realizing. They shake their heads.

                    MARCUS
          Lara?

Waiting. SILENCE.

EXT. THE DOME - NIGHT

BEDLAM. The CROWD ask questions, complain, refuse to budge.
Lara pushes through, listening for info - OVERHEARS -

                         BLACK MALE REPORTER
                    (to camera)
          - the cause is unknown, but eye
          witnesses claim that it happened
          the exact moment the players were
          killed in the game. How that can
          happen is, as yet, unclear -

                         CAUCASIAN FEMALE REPORTER
          This game launch has gone from a
          golden ticket to a bloody nightmare
          as a number of participants have
          been hospitalized. What has aptly
          been renamed by those present as
          'the Terrordome', has been closed
          off to spectators and media -

                         ASIAN MALE REPORTER
          - a shocking turn of events where
          the most eagerly anticipated launch
          in the history of gaming has become
          the most catastrophic. So certain
          of its success, Tom Niko allowed
          widespread media coverage, but
          instead of valuable publicity has
          obtained a PR disaster -

                         OLD CAUCASIAN REPORTER
          - anticipate word from Mr. Niko who
          has been very vocal until just a
          few moments ago -
                    (touches earpiece)
          I'm getting word now that two
          gamers have in fact died -

                         YOUNG LATINO REPORTER
          Did you see what happened?

                         KID'S DAD
          Gamer Nine was having some kind of
          seizure in his chair.

                         YOUNG LATINO REPORTER
          Do you think it was directly
          connected to the game?

                         KID'S DAD
                    (guilt-stricken)
          Looked that way. But I hope not, my
          son is one of the -

Suddenly he is dragged away by TWO SECURITY OFFICERS -

                    KID'S DAD
          Hey, get your hands off me!

Lara quickens her step to keep from losing them. Kid's Dad is
taken back inside The Dome through a side door. Lara is
brusquely stopped -

                    LARA
          I'm with him.

The SECURITY at the door shakes his head.

                    LARA (CONT'D)
          I am! Where am I supposed to go?

                    SECURITY
               (points randomly)
          Away.

With a HUFF Lara mooches off back amongst the outraged crowd,
in search of a familiar face. Her eyes roam anxiously.

The TUMULTUOUS PROTESTS from the crowd grow as flashing red
and blue lights arrive on the periphery.

Shoving his microphone in people's face -

                    BLACK MALE REPORTER
          What did you see inside The Dome?

A light bulb moment, Lara pushes through -

                    LARA
          I saw everything. When the players
          were killed in the game, they were
          in real life too.

                    BLACK MALE REPORTER
          How?

Lara notices The Two Security Officers have their eye on her.
The more she says the closer they come -

                    LARA
          And before the evacuation, players
          were trying to exit the game and
          couldn't. I think they're trap -

The Two Security Guards strong-arm the Reporter and drag Lara
away. She goes willingly as they take her through the same
side door of The Dome.

INT. TOM NIKO'S PLUSH EXECUTIVE BOX

Coming undone, drinking and snorting cocaine, Tom paces back
and forth, watching the CHAOS beneath him.

Desperate to please -

                    NANCY
          Maybe they had underlying health
          problems. People don't always
          disclose things.

                    TOM NIKO
          That would work. Call Ace to find
          out where we'd stand legally -

As Nancy obediently dabs at the sweat on Tom's brow a
THUNDEROUS RAPPING at the door makes him jump.

Nina enters.

                    NINA
          Oh God!!
              (he's worse than she even
               expected)
          We need you.

She cannot believe she is even saying it. Tom's face is like
- *Oh, shit!*

                    NINA (CONT'D)
          I may do pretty much everything
          around here, but I'm no good at
          impressions. Since you're Tom Niko.
          The genius! You probably know how
          to fix this already! Right?

She rolls her eyes and leaves.

                    NINA (O.S.) (CONT'D)
          Don't make me call you publicly.

INT. MAZE OF VENTS (LEVEL 3)

Crawling in single file Kid, Six, Marcus then -

                    THIRTEEN
          This is either a really good idea,
          or a really, REALLY bad one.

                    SIX
          I barely fit.

                    KID
          Shit! Dead end.

They are forced to shuffle backwards.

                    THIRTEEN
          Stop, stop!

A pile-up ensues. Pushing Marcus's foot out of his face -

                    THIRTEEN (CONT'D)
          Shit, I heard something.
               (squeaking)
          Something else is in here! Go!!

GUNFIRE.

                    THIRTEEN (CONT'D)
          Wait! Stop! DON'T SHOOT!! I've been
          shot once already.

                    SEVEN (O.S.)
               (nervous; barely audible)
          Hello?

All let out a COLLECTIVE SIGH.

INT. PLUSH GREEN ROOM

Lara is manhandled and dumped in a chair. Rubbing her now
sore arms -

                    LARA
          There was no need for that. Wait,
          you're just going to leave me
          here!?

They SLAM the door behind them, lock it. Lara turns around -

                    LARA (CONT'D)
          You! Who are you?

It's Kid's Dad.

Lara sees the Friendly Security Guard through the door's
small window - BANGS for attention -

EXT. EMPTY FOYER

The Friendly Security Guard stops and looks. MUFFLED behind
the thick glass -

                    LARA
          Hey! Remember me?

She waves at him and mimes pleading with clenched hands . He
looks around - approaches. Jumping for joy -

                    LARA (CONT'D)
          Yes!

INT. CORRIDOR

Kid falls out of a wall vent. Six scrambles out with the
agility of someone half his age and size - he feels his
pants. Thirteen is next, his eyeline level with Six's crotch -

                    THIRTEEN
          What are you doing?

                    SIX
          I feel wet.

But he isn't. Six shakes the thought, the fear and dread on
his face fade slightly.

                    SEVEN (O.S.)
          What's the holdup! Let me out.

INT. GAMERS CIRCLE

Six's lap *is* wet. At some point he has pissed himself in
fear. The Floor Manager passes by scribbling on her tablet.
The Friendly Security Guard approaches, escorting -

                    FLOOR MANAGER
          Lara, is it? This better be good.

Rushing past her straight to -

                    LARA
          Marcus, are you okay?

                    FLOOR MANAGER
          Who's this?

                    KIDS'S DAD
          Player 19, I'm his Father.

Floor Manager glares at the Friendly Security Guard - *He
Cannot be here!*

                    FRIENDLY SECURITY GUARD
          He was talking to the media. Plus,
          he's already seen the worst of it.

                    FLOOR MANAGER
          I wouldn't bet on it.
               (to Kid's Dad)
          I'm sorry but you really can't be
          here.

Friendly Security Guard's WALKIE-TALKIE SOUNDS and he dashes
off -

                    KID'S DAD
          Two gamers have been taken out on
          stretchers - I'm not going anywhere
          until you tell me what is going on.

He hands over a business card - He's a Lawyer. That's all she
needs. Floor Manager looks up, past Kid's Dad -

                    FLOOR MANAGER
          Ah, you can see *him* about that.

Tom Niko has finally returned. Floor Manager shoves past him.

Nearby, looking at the other active screens, as she WHISPERS
into comatose Marcus's ear over the CHAOS -

                    LARA
          - I'll tell you what's been
          happening here, but first we need
          to make sure you'll be safe enough
          to stop and listen.

                    KID (ON TV)
              (ecstatic)
          She's back!?

Floor Manager's mouth falls open.

INT. GALLERY

Fingers fly across the keyboard.

                    NINA
              (it dawns on her)
          Tom should never have signed off on
          our top programmers and strategists
          going into the game on opening
          night.

                    VISION MIXER
          You knew.

                    NINA
          I don't claim to be a genius. We
          needed someone in there, but there
          were plenty others willing -

Floor Manager BURSTS in to the COMMOTION already going on.

                    FLOOR MANAGER
          Come out here. You'll want to see
          this. Everyone.

She leaves just as fast as she came.

INT. GAMERS CIRCLE

The bewildered gaggle of Production Staff enter. Floor
Manager beckons them over to Lara, next to Marcus. They
MURMUR questioningly -

                    FLOOR MANAGER
          Shhhh!

They watch Lara SPEAK INSTRUCTIONS in Marcus's ear.

                    LARA
          We're gonna help keep you all safe
          until the issues are fixed.

Marcus relays this info -

                    KID (ON TV)
          Cool. Tell them to hurry.

                    LARA
          No need, you just did.

The Production Staff are stunned by the back and forth
exchange.

                    NINA
                (to the team)
          How have we never known about the
          sound bleed into the game?

Three slinks past Lara with a sarcastic sneer as he joins Tom
and the team.

                    LARA
          What's the cheat doing here?

                    SIX (ON TV)
          I hear voices now. What are they
          saying?

                    TOM NIKO
          They heard us!?

Lara gives Three a "what the fuck" look.

                    THREE
                (surprised himself)
          Well, during testing we were in
          small, quiet rooms with no more
          that ten people. And on-site
          testing had minimal staff too.

The penny drops -

                    LARA
          He works for you!? But he was -

Nina looks to Tom to answer. Sweaty and fidgety - his God-like air completely evaporated -

                    TOM NIKO
          We needed experienced players to
          look out for gamers on the inside.

                    NINA
          Well, that's *part* of it.

Tom doesn't seem to grasp her meaning. Up close, Lara's adoration has instantaneously evaporated.

                    LARA
          How'd that work out for you? *He*
          [Three] shot a player in the back!

Tom feigns surprise, unable to talk his way out.

                    LARA (CONT'D)
          Don't look like that. You saw
          yourself! On the super-massive
          screen right there. I know, because
          I watched you watching.
               (Tom stares, slack-jawed)
          I guess maybe you just forgot. It's
          been a busy night after all. And
          with that mind of yours going a
          hundred miles an hour 24/7. By the
          way, you have something on your
          nose.

Tom wipes at the white powder. Lara goes back to Marcus to pick up where she left off. Seething, Tom BARKS angrily -

                    TOM NIKO
          Who is this girl? What's she even
          doing here? Get her out!

                    NINA
          No. She's helping. If it weren't
          for her we'd not know how to
          communicate with those in the game.

Tom turns his anger towards Kid's Dad-

                    TOM NIKO
          You, why are you here?

                    KID'S DAD
          I'm a lawyer -

                    TOM NIKO
          Oh! Good, over here.

                    NINA
          He's not one of yours. He's with
          them [the gamers].

Livid, Tom turns to his verbal punching bag - Nancy. She
clears her throat uncomfortably -

                    TOM NIKO
               (QUIET; venomous)
          Get rid of him.
               (Before she can ask how)
          I don't care how, just do it.

She obediently skulks off, signalling Kid's Dad to follow.
Taking him by the arm -

                    NANCY
          Please, follow me.

Tom shoos him away condescendingly. Kid's Dad bristles.

                    FLOOR MANAGER
          You had employees participating?
          Care to mention that to me!?

                    TOM NIKO
          It was strictly need to know.

                    FLOOR MANAGER
          Well know this. I quit!

She shoves her headgear at him -

                    FLOOR MANAGER (CONT'D)
          Since you're back I won't be needed
          anymore. After all, what do I know!

She walks out. Tom seethes in SILENCE - looks for -

                    NINA
          Nancy's busy already. Remember.

Nina takes the equipment - if looks could kill.

INT. COMMS CENTRE

TALKING OVER ONE ANOTHER in their panic -

                    KID
          Shhh!

Terror crosses Marcus's face as he listens.

                    THE OTHERS
          What?

                    MARCUS
          Some of the gamers -

                    THIRTEEN
          They're dead aren't they.

                              SIX
                    Make them tell us everything. Now!

INT. GAMERS CIRCLE

Suddenly, panic surrounds another gamer -

EXT. THE DOME - NIGHT

The huge crowd still refuse to leave, CHANTING 'Let us
in/Tell the truth'. Security are outnumbered, despite backup.

INT. CORRIDOR

Two limps past numerous doors, gun at the ready. The door is
open to a -

INT. CABIN

Stepping through the doorway, Two is faced with the barrel of
a gun -

                         TWO
                    (cowering)
               Don't!

                         ONE (O.S)
               Alyx!?
                    (lowers his weapon)
               You're still here!

                         TWO
               Only just.

She is in a lot of pain. One tosses over a medikit. Two knows
exactly what to do.

                         ONE
               You heard from control?

Two shakes her head.

                         TWO
               Any others left?

One shrugs.

                         TWO (CONT'D)
               Have you tried to exit?

One shakes his head - *Why would he?*

                    TWO (CONT'D)
          I wonder what's happening out
          there.

                    ONE
          Don't bother. We're in here.

                    TWO
          I've not been able to find any
          supplies.

                    ONE
          But the -

                    TWO
          Weapons store is down the hall.

She nods then shakes her head. One is puzzled.

                    TWO (CONT'D)
          It's worse than our worst case
          scenario.

                    ONE
          Yep.

INT. GAMERS CIRCLE

Leaning in, Nina murmurs in Two's ear -

                    NINA
          Alyx.

The screen in front of the stationary gamer jolts.

                    TWO (O.S)
          You're back online!

                    NINA
          Not exactly, but we'll have
          instructions soon, hang in there.
               (SHOUTS OVER TO)
          Max!

Three hightails it over. Eyeing him dubiously -

                    LARA
               (in Marcus's ear)
          Just give me a minute.

Three crouches by One and WHISPERS in his ear. Again, the
screen jolts in response.

Nina returns to Tom, WHISPERING - Nina doing most of the
spitballing. Lara approaches -

                    NINA
          We need all gamers together in the
          game. Everyone needs to be on the -

                    TOM NIKO
               (copying)
          - be on the same page. Right! Pool
          our ideas.

As Lara steps closer -

                    NINA
          You!

                    LARA
          It's Lara.

                    NINA
          Right, yeah, Lara. All the gamers
          need to be guided to -

                    TOM NIKO
               (to everyone)
          Guide gamers to the Med Bay.
               (off her questioning look)
          It's the most central for all
          gamers left. Guide the group there.

                    LARA
          What then?

Tom looks to Nina -

                    NINA
          We'll get to that.

They don't know yet.

                    LARA
          There are five gamers together
          already in the Comms Centre. It'd
          be safer to keep them there and
          lead the others to them.

                    NINA
               (careful contemplation)
          She's right.

                    TOM NIKO
               (reluctantly)
          Fine.

                    NINA
               (SHOUTS across the room)
          Get the gamers to the Comms Centre,
          not the Med Bay.

                    THREE
          Why?

                    NINA
          Just do it Max!
               (ANNOUNCES)
          We need medics keeping a close eye
          on gamers, monitoring anything and
          everything. Find them.

We see what she describes - The strain of the last forty
minutes already showing as the Four Medics hurry towards One
and Two first.

                    NINA (CONT'D)
               (back to Tom)
          Now all we need is more ideas for
          possible solutions. We only have
          these so far.

Nina hands Tom a Post-it so there aren't many. Tom clearly
has absolutely nothing more to add.

                    NINA (CONT'D)
          These depend on getting willing
          volunteers to actually try them.

Lara takes a deep calming breath in the insanity around her.
Softens with trepidation -

                    LARA
          Why is all this even happening?

          TOM NIKO   NINA
We're looking into it.   They're looking into it.

Nina points to the Production Staff huddle, mind mapping.
They cross out most of the ideas they come up with. Lara
looks over with sad optimism.

On numerous TV screens we see gamers being led safely through
the maze of corridors by the people crouched next to their
comatose bodies in the real world, WHISPERING in their ear.

                    THREE
          No!

Four is agonisingly torn apart on screen, his entrails pulled
out in POV shot. Three sits in his old seat, holds his head
in his hands. Heading way back to Marcus, Lara passes Three -

                    LARA
               (sincerely)
          One of your work friends? Sorry.

Three turns away and wipes his face. Moves to One and Two.
Sitting by Marcus -

                    LARA (CONT'D)
          Marcus, the other gamers are coming
          to you. There's a few things you
          need to know.

INT. COMMS CENTRE

Six twists uncomfortably in his pants -

                    SIX
          How many got out alive?

                    MARCUS
          They won't say.

Everyone is asking questions at once.

          THIRTEEN   KID
What are they doing to get us   How many Monsters are left?
out?

                    SIX
          He's trying to tell us. Just shut
          up and listen!

Trying to remain calm -

                    MARCUS
          Other gamers are being led to us.
          Programmers are working on how to
          get us out. We just have to stay,
          alive.

                    THIRTEEN
          Easier said than done.
             (Six stares him down)
          What? It's the truth.

                    MARCUS
          There are no more supplies anywhere
          in the game, weapons or medikits.
          It all disappeared. Whatever we do,
          wherever we go, we need to be as
          careful as if it were real life. If
          we die in the game -

Expectant SILENCE.

                    KID
          We die for real?

Kid is crestfallen, starts to WEEP.

                    THIRTEEN
          That's it, we're done for.

                    KID
          I'm too young to die.

                    SIX
          Kid, we all are.

                    KID
          I shouldn't even really be here.
          I'm thirteen.

The others look to Thirteen, confused a moment.

                    KID (CONT'D)
          I'm thirteen years old.

The gravity of his words hang in the air. Six tries to
comfort him -

                    SIX
          Hey Kid, we're all in this
          together.

INT. GAMERS CIRCLE

A CLOUD OF WHISPERS as everyone stops - turns to the screen -

                    TOM NIKO
          What did he say?

                    NINA
          This just goes from bad to worse.

                    LARA
             (SHOUTS over)
          Nobody pays attention to the age
          limits on games. Just like nobody
          would have thought something like
          this would ever happen.

                    TOM NIKO
             (to Nina; scheming)
          So the Lawyer's kid is underage.

Tom mulls over how he can use this to his advantage. Nina
ignores him - on the big screen One and Two are battling
against four Creatures.

Something catches Lara's eye on another screen -

                    LARA
             (sotto)
          What the hell?
             (hurrying to Seven's side)
          Hey, what are you doing? Everyone
          is on their way to the Comms
          Centre.

                    SEVEN
          Who's that!?

                    LARA
          I'm in the Dome, I'm a substitute.
          You need to rejoin the group.

                    SEVEN
          What do you know, sub. I'd rather
          go it alone.

                    LARA
          You can't just hide and you really
          aren't better alone right now.
          Please, let me help you get back.

INT. COMMS CENTRE

                    THIRTEEN
          I hear something!

                    SIX
          Please be another gamer.

                    MARCUS
          Where's Seven?

                    KID
          It must to be her.

Kid is about to shout out when Thirteen covers his mouth.

                    SIX
                 (WHISPERS)
          We can't take any chances.

Six shuts the door - a BOOMING on the other side. Six signals
for them to be quiet and hide, weapons aimed.

INT. GAMERS CIRCLE

Production Staff look up at the COMMOTION -

                    TOM NIKO
          They should have moved to the Med
          Bay like I said.

                    LARA
          There's always going to be
          something coming for them
          eventually wherever they are.

Seven's screen goes dark until she comes to a hatch above.

INT. COMMS CENTRE

All is momentarily QUIET.

                    KID
          It went away.

Marcus, Six, Kid and Thirteen spin round at the sound of
METAL ON METAL from within the room. Against his better
judgement, Marcus crawls closer -

                    KID (CONT'D)
          What are you doing!

Marcus realizes its Seven and helps yank the maintenance
hatch open. Seven climbs out.

                    THIRTEEN
          You! Again!!

                    SEVEN
          What! Ahhh -

She flinches uncontrollably and FIRES. Everyone hits the
deck. She drops her gun. Thirteen lunges -

                    THIRTEEN
          You!
               (Marcus holds him back)
          You could have killed us!

Thinking they are all simply overreacting -

                    SEVEN
          I didn't. Stop whining.

She rubs her finger as she goes for her gun - flinches again,
making everyone jump for cover. Thirteen aims at her.

                    THIRTEEN
          Do not reach for that again!

INT. GAMERS CIRCLE

A heart monitor is attached to Seven's finger.

In the B.G. another gamer nearby is taken away on a stretcher
by Security as Medics check Seven's heart rate and breathing.

Six and Thirteen' are next and their heart-rates skyrocket.
The medics watch the screens open-mouthed.

As the Forth Medic starts on Kid, he flails and SCREAMS as if
some invisible thing is on him. Weapons go off and are
dropped unintentionally. Six grabs his chest.

                    LARA
          Stop touching them! They can feel
          everything -

                    NINA
               (off the Medics' confused
                looks)
          Goddammit, you need to talk them
          through what you're about to do.

                    MEDIC
          But they're unconscious.

                    LARA
               (at the end of her tether)
          Watch.

She jabs Marcus in the side -

                    MARCUS (ON TV)
          Arghhh!

And he reacts on screen. She leans in -

                    LARA
          Marcus, it's only me. Tell them not
          to panic.

                    SIX (ON TV)
          I can't take any more of this. I'm
          feeling things that aren't there,
          in a spaceship that's not even
          real, with monsters that might
          actually kill me.

Astonished, a Medic copies Lara's action with Seven. His
actions affect what she does on screen. Finally getting it.

                    NINA
          Wait, why aren't the others
          connected up to your monitors? And
          where are the rest of you?

                    MEDIC
          We don't have the equipment for
          them all at once. There's only four
          of us. They're fine [One and Two]
          we just checked them.

                    NINA
          It's a 50,000 capacity stadium!

The Medic shrugs. Nina looks to Tom Niko --

                    TOM NIKO
          It didn't seem necessary for such a
          safe and innovative -

His voice trails off.

                    LARA
          You need to call 911.

          TOM NIKO   NINA
Now hang on, there must be   They'd never get through the
another -   crowd out there.

INT. COMMS CENTRE

The weird sensations subside to everyone's relief. They look
to Marcus expectantly.

A clear yet distant sounding voice is heard by everyone -

                    LARA (O.S.)
          Don't panic, the strange sensations
          are medics checking your vitals.

          NINETEEN   MARCUS
Is that --   Lara.

                    SIX
          Jeez, could my nerves be any more
          shot!?

                    THIRTEEN
          Do not pick up that gun. If you do
          I shoot you!

                    SEVEN
          Overreact much!

                    MARCUS
          Please, be careful.

                    SEVEN
          What does it even matter!?

                    SIX
          Believe me, it matters!

                    KID
          You left us. Again!!

                    SEVEN
          So!

                    SIX
          Where were you?

                    SEVEN
          Not far away, looking for ammo.

Thirteen rolls his eyes -

                THIRTEEN   KID
    Hiding more like.   Don't you listen!?

                         SIX
              You can't just wander off.
              Something is seriously wrong.

                         SEVEN
                    (mock fear)
              Yeah, we're on an alien infested
              spaceship. I know!

                         MARCUS
              Wait, she doesn't know.

                         KID
              Are you gonna stick with us or run
              and hide again when shit gets real?

    Seven doesn't have an answer. Too proud to admit she's
    petrified.

                         THIRTEEN
              I don't think we should tell her.
              Lets set her loose to find out for
              herself. We don't have time to
              explain. She's a liability.

                         SEVEN
              And you're a dick. Shutting the
              door on me. Had to crawl in a
              filthy tunnel to get back.

    The others exchange looks, unsure how to word it.

                         KID
              When you die here you're dead for
              real.

    Seven LAUGHS dismissively. Sees they are deadly serious, but
    still doesn't quite get it -

                         MARCUS
              We can't 'EXIT GAME!'

    Seven's face drops.

                         LARA (O.S.)
              Change of plan people, someone else
              is in trouble -

                         SIX
                    (sotto)
              Aren't we all.

                         LARA (O.S.)
               You need to get down to the next
               level. You'll have to use your
               weapons, but try not to.

They go to the door. As it opens they are faced with a WINGED-
WEIRDO. Kid instantly shuts the door again.

                         THIRTEEN
               So how do we get out of here?

Looking to the hatch. Six is not pleased.

INT. GAMERS CIRCLE

Nina scribbles a route on some blueprints and hands it to
Lara.

                         NINA
               They trust you.

                         LARA
               Take the third right, should be
               about 150 feet.

INT. MAINTENANCE TUNNEL

Crouching, but still able to walk, in single file they take
the third right.

                         SIX
               This is manageable.

                         LARA (O.S.)
               Take the next left.

As they do they hear a distant SCREECHING. Panic! They pick
up speed.

                         LARA (O.S.) (CONT'D)
               Take a left, and the second right.

The SCREECHING is closer -

                         MARCUS
               The hatch!

INT. CORRIDOR TO SERVER ROOM

Six is last to climb out.

                         SIX
               Who has the most ammo right now?

They make way for Seven to take the lead -

                    SEVEN
          Here.

She shares out her weapons and ammo.

                    KID
          Oh, so now you want to share.

                    THIRTEEN
          Just accept it.
               (to Kid)
          Better we get some before she runs
          and hides again.

As they join the fray, a Creature (AN AMALGAMATION OF THREE
DIFFERENT THINGS) is half way through to the Servers, having
SMASHED it's way in, and takes gunfire from both sides.

                    TWO
          A little help please!

Marcus FIRES first, carefully, into the main body of the
Creature -

                    ONE
          Everyone aim for the body, or head
          if you see it.

                    THIRTEEN
               (To Seven)
          You're wasting ammo, hit the body,
          not the legs.

                    SEVEN
          It'll slow it down.

                    SIX
          It'll just change and come back!

Seven hits the body. They begin to run out of ammo.

                    ONE
          Don't stop. We've almost got it,
          keep going.

Seven has a grenade -

                    THIRTEEN
          You had that all along?

Marcus snatches it -

                    SEVEN
          Hey!

It finally takes the Creature out. Smoke billows -

                    TWO
          Are you okay in there?

SUB FOURTEEN climbs over the Creature.

                    KID
          Who's that?

INT. MED BAY (LEVEL 2)

Everyone finally gathered together.

                    THIRTEEN
          So this is it!?

                    SIX
          There's nobody else?

Marcus, One and Two shake their heads.

                    MARCUS
          You the only Kagami Gaming
          employees left?

Everyone else is stupefied.

          TWO   THIRTEEN
Didn't I say, people would   What!
figure it out.

                    ONE
               (reluctant)
          There *were* four of us.

                    SIX
          Why?

                    TWO
               (sheepish)
          To try and make the launch go more
          smoothly.

                    SIX
          So can you explain what the hell is
          going on?

                    ONE
          Maybe too many players exited the
          game. The AI has overridden the
          controls to keep the game going. I
          think. That, or it figures trapping
          us is a good scare tactic. Anyone
          here claustrophobic? [Six for sure]
          I told him it wasn't ready yet.

                    MARCUS
          Who?

                    TWO   ONE
We can't stand around
chatting, we could be
attacked any minute. We can
explain when we get out.   -- Tom can.

                         TWO
               First of all who needs ammo?

'Me's' and raised hands all round.

Two and One share their own out. Seven is particularly quiet -

                    TWO (CONT'D)
               How you doing for supplies?

                         SEVEN
               Fine.

          THIRTEEN   TWO
You have more!?   What you got?

                    SEVEN (CONT'D)
               What's it to you?

One grabs Seven's watch -

                    SEVEN (CONT'D)
               Hey!

                         ONE
               Two medikits and five rounds.

He proceeds to take it and toss it to those that need it.

                         SEVEN
               You can't do that, it's mine! If
               they have none too bad, they'll
               have to get their own.

                         SIX
               There is no more.

One finds three grenades in Seven's inventory, keeps one,
tosses another to Two. Looks around and chooses -

                         ONE
               You.

- Marcus for the third.

                    ONE (CONT'D)
               I know who you are, you're one of
               the best at first-person shooters.
               Now, how to get out of this.

                    THIRTEEN
               Couldn't we just be unplugged?

                    ONE
          Only the player is supposed to -

                    SIX
          The rules went out the window way
          back though.

                    ONE
          Does anyone outside have anything?

                    THREE (O.S.)
          Nothing guaranteed Theo -

                    TWO
          Suicide!?
               (off the shocked faces)
          The game killed the others. Maybe
          if we do it ourself it will work
          like exiting the game.

Two looks to One for approval - torn, he isn't confident.

                    MARCUS
          Please, don't.

                    SEVEN
          It's worth a shot.

                    MARCUS
          Is it? Maybe we just need to
          complete the game. It's what we're
          good at, right?!

Marcus speaks up so little it takes them all by surprise.

                    SEVEN
          That's impossible.

                    MARCUS
          Maybe not. If we work together.

                    SEVEN
          Where's Tom Niko? What does he
          think

One and Two look away.

INT. GAMERS CIRCLE

Tom gives a stern look, refusing to speak. Lara turns to
Nina -

                    LARA
          Do you think suicide could work?

She shrugs, curious herself.

                    NINA
          It's one of the few things we
          thought of too. It's risky, but so
          is everything else.

INT. MED BAY

                    KID
          Go ahead. Try it.

All but Marcus and One look on in SILENT anticipation. To
everyone, but mainly One -

                    TWO
          It's worth a try.

                    ONE
          You sure about this?

Two shrugs, shares out her ammo and weapons.

                    MARCUS
          What are you doing?

Keeps a single bullet for herself -

                    TWO
          Just in case.

Two only hesitates a moment. POP! She hits the floor.
Everyone reels in horror. Unmoving, blood oozing.

Marcus and Thirteen turn her over -

                    ONE
          Stop. It's useless.

                    MARCUS
          But -

                    ONE
             (regretful)
          We can't do anything for her in
          here.

Unable to bear the SILENCE -

                    MARCUS
          Lara?

INT. GAMERS CIRCLE

An excruciating pause. A Medic checks for Two's pulse. Shakes
her head regretfully.

INT. MED BAY

An expectant beat.

                    LARA (O.S.)
          It didn't work.

Everyone stands in mournful SILENCE.

                    KID
          Oh my God I told her -

Six puts a reassuring arm round Kid. Sub Fourteen is
traumatized, just managing to hold it together.

                    ONE
          Next idea.
               (off the disgusted looks)
          You want out of here, we need to
          try something else.
               (off the SILENCE)
          Someone mentioned unplugging from
          the outside -

                    SEVEN
          Yeah, I was thinking that too.

LONG SILENCE.

                    SUB FOURTEEN
          Then who's gonna try?

                    ONE
          I will.

                    MARCUS
          No!
               (surprising everyone)
          He knows the game better than
          anyone else here. We need him.

                    ONE
          I don't know what the rules are
          anymore. This is as risky as the
          last idea. And I can't guarantee
          I'd be of much more use.

                    SIX
          Twenty's right.

Looking round for someone else to volunteer.

                    MARCUS
          If its so risky, let's risk playing
          the game. Won't those odds be
          better?

                    SEVEN
          I'll try.

Marcus's expression implores her to rethink.

                    SEVEN (CONT'D)
          I'd rather die now than have this
          be my reality for who knows how
          long. I've hated every second of
          it. I like games, on a screen, its
          the not being realistic that I love
          about them. I just want out.

They all wait a painfully long time -

                    SEVEN (CONT'D)
                (to the real world)
          Hello! What's going on? Unplug me.

Still no answer -

                    LARA (O.S.)
          They're trying to convince someone
          to do it.

                    MARCUS
          See, they think it's a bad idea.

                    SEVEN
          I want Tom Niko to.

As if that will make everything work out.

INT. GAMERS CIRCLE

                    LARA
          It makes sense, it's his game,
          right!?

Tom looks around for a way out, meets eyes with Three -

                    TOM NIKO
          You. You do it.

Three looks to Nina for help -

          NINA   TOM NIKO
You don't have to -   If he wants to keep his job
                            he does.

                    NANCY (O.C.)
          I'll do it.
             (looking terrified)
          You'll have to show me how.

                    TOM NIKO
          Where's the Kid's father?

Nancy points up to the Executive box -

                    TOM NIKO (CONT'D)
          You're letting him watch!?

                    NANCY
          He can't hear. I called Ace -

          TOM NIKO   NANCY
My Lawyer!?   I didn't know what else to
   (thinks again)   do.
Good, good. Good call.

Nancy breathes a sigh of relief. Nina waits to show her what
to do.

                    SEVEN (ON TV)
          Hello! Is anything happening?

Nina urges Tom to speak up, Lara hands him the mic -

                    TOM NIKO
          We're just, uh, getting prepared.

His voice reverberates around the almost empty stadium.

                    SEVEN (ON TV)
          Oh my God, Tom Niko, I love you!

Nina gives Tom a thumbs up -

                    TOM NIKO
          We're ready when you are.

His attempt at being chipper is ill-timed.

                    SEVEN
          Ready. Oh my God I cannot wait to
          meet you.

                    TOM NIKO
          Okay in 3, 2, 1.

Nancy unplugs Seven who remains motionless in the chair. The
Medic looks for signs of life - grabs a defibrillator.

Lara can't watch. Looks back at Marcus's POV, looking down at
Seven still present within the game -

INT. MED BAY

Seven spasms as if possessed.

                    LARA (O.S.)
          Don't touch her! They're trying to
          revive her.

Marcus pulls Sub Fourteen further back.

INT. GAMERS CIRCLE

The Medic steps back. It hasn't worked. MOANS OF
DISAPPOINTMENT and HOPELESSNESS all around.

                    LARA
               (WHISPERS)
          What now?

Nobody has an answer. Avoiding everyone's gaze -

                    TOM NIKO
          Shit.

Their SILENCE allows the outside CHANTING to seep through.

                    LARA
          What's that noise?

                    NINA
          The spectators outside. They won't
          leave. Backup is on its way.

                    LARA
          Backup, from where?

EXT. THE DOME - NIGHT

The crowd and the UPROAR is growing as the Police arrive.

INT. MED BAY

All is quiet - only DISTANT CHATTER, like WHISPERS. The group
place the bodies of Two and Seven respectfully on beds, each
wrapped in a blanket.

                    SIX
          Are the medics still working on us?

                    THIRTEEN
          I don't feel anything.

                    SIX
          It's like there's something wrapped
          tight around my [left] arm.

                    THIRTEEN
          They must be then.

                    SIX
          Hey Kid, gimme that medikit.

                    KID
          Its the last one.

                    THIRTEEN
          No, you're not injured!

Kid doesn't know what to do. Six snatches it from him.

                    SIX
          I feel like shit.

                    THIRTEEN
          You are pretty old.

                    SIX
          And yet in this world I'm faster
          and stronger than you.

He uses it, but it has no effect.

                    MARCUS
          Sit, rest. Lara said they're
          keeping an eye on us.

As Six does so.

                    THIRTEEN
               (remembers)
          Wait a second, he already is.

They all have to think a moment.

                    ONE
          Do you still hear us out there?

                    LARA (O.S.)
          They hear you, they're discussing.
          The options.

                    ONE
          We don't have time for any more
          talking, we need action.

                    THIRTEEN
          Instead of unplugging players,
          unplug the game. That's the source
          of the problem, right!?

INT. GAMERS CIRCLE

In QUIET CONFAB Nina tries to encourage Tom to take charge -

                    LARA
          It's being discussed right now.

In the background we see the Four Medics are still busy with
Two and Seven. Nobody is checking on the others right now!

                    NINA
          It's that or get them to complete
          the game.

Tom paces without answering.

                    NINA (CONT'D)
          Can you think of anything better?
          You've been pretty quiet.

                    TOM NIKO
          I can't just come up with solutions
          like that [SNAPS his fingers]. I'm
          not a performing monkey.

                    NINA
               (under her breath)
          Could have fooled me.

Tom and Nina are nose to nose. Already on the defensive Tom's
instinct is to explode. It takes every ounce of his strength
to show restraint, especially as he is being watched. He
backs down.

          TOM NIKO   MARCUS (ON TV)
Fine.   Wait, we should take a vote!

Nina follows TOM to the mains, amongst the cables, she points
out the biggest one.

          TOM NIKO   ONE
       (impatient)   Stop! We never agreed.
I know, I can do it.

Confusion as what seemed at first to be a discussion, appears
to actually be taking place. The Gamers hurriedly vote and
only Thirteen and Sub Fourteen hesitantly vote to unplug.

                    LARA
          Wait! They all need to agree.

Production Staff add to the utter chaos by VOCALIZING their
dissent too. All the while Tom reaches for the cable,
tightens his grip. He takes a deep breath - an agonizing
internal battle going on - completely oblivious to everything
else.

                    ALL GAMERS
          STOP, DON'T, WE'RE GONNA PLAY!

Nina realizes and grabs his hand -

          NINA   TOM NIKO
You idiot. We didn't mean do   You can't talk to me like
it right away!   that!

Nina catches her breath - contemplates -

                    NINA
          We weren't ready to launch.

                    TOM NIKO
               (anger bubbling)
          Everyone was waiting for the next
          big thing.

                    NINA
          And you're probably the only person
          on the planet able to make people
          wait longer. So why wouldn't you!?
               (the words don't come)
          Power, that's why. Power and money.
          Only reason I stayed is I remember
          when you weren't like, this.

This is a hard pill for Tom to finally swallow.

                    LARA
          Its okay guys, it's under control.

                    SIX
          Sounds pretty far from that.

INT. MED BAY

                    THIRTEEN
          So we could have all died together,
          but instead we get to die
          separately. One by one. Great.

                    SUB FOURTEEN
          It might even have worked! Is he
          [Thirteen] always this negative.

Marcus, Kid and Six nod.

                    SIX
          How do we even play a game like
          this? Wasn't it a battle royale?
          That means only one of us can
          survive.

                    ONE
               (not too convincing)
          If we just play, it may ease up on
          us and let us out. It all started
          when everyone was exiting.

An INDECIPHERABLE TAP/SCRATCH/FLAP noise passes outside. They
already have their guns at the ready.

INT. WIDE CORRIDOR FROM MED BAY

They don't waste any time getting as much distance between themselves and the NOISE as possible. Whatever it is, it moves fast -

                    MARCUS
          Where should we be heading?

                    ONE
          Away from that noise.

One leads the way with purpose.

                    MARCUS
          What is it?

One shrugs. He speaks with dark intensity -

                    ONE
          What it is is irrelevant. We need
          to keep away from everything.

Eyes to the ceiling, he stops to open a panel that reveals a ladder. They proceed to CLIMB it one-by-one. Six sees a huge WINGED CREATURE fly past the end of the corridor. Eye widen with dread -

                    SIX
          Hurry.

Marcus ascends next. As he turns back to help he sees Six GASPING FOR BREATH -

                    MARCUS
          Six!

Six grips his arm and slumps to the ground -

                    THIRTEEN
          Six! Come on, let me help you.

                    SIX
          I can't.

The others circle him. He sees the Winged Creature now headed their way.

                    SIX (CONT'D)
          Go. I'll catch up.

Sub Fourteen looks up and tears off out of sight.

                    THIRTEEN
          Hey, we need to stick together!

                    SIX
          Just go! It's alright.

Thirteen has to drag Kid away. They hate to leave him behind but comply.

INT. NARROW STAIRCASE

Slipping and scrambling like in a nightmare, Kid and Thirteen hit the stairs. As they reach the top the Winged Creature grabs Kid by the leg. Thirteen grabs him and a tug of war ensues. Kid YELPS IN PAIN AND TERROR. Thirteen won't let go but clearly cannot win either.

Kicking and squirming, Kid pries a hand free and grapples for his gun.

A RATTLE OF GUNFIRE.

Thirteen and Kid fall back.

Marcus and One keep FIRING - the Creature scarpers.

INT. GAMERS CIRCLE

Six is painfully rigid in his seat. The defibrillator no longer working. It has no charge left.

                    MEDIC
          We have to move him.

All Four take action.

INT. FLIGHT DECK

Thirteen and Marcus help Kid into a chair.

                    MARCUS
          You gonna be alright?

                    THIRTEEN
          He has to be.

He is clearly in pain.

                    ONE
          Just remember, this is all in your
          head. Your leg is perfectly fine in
          reality.

Kid nods but his face says otherwise.

                    THIRTEEN
          Guys, security images!

Thirteen looks at various areas - dead bodies in some, Creatures of various shapes and sizes, others deserted.

                         KID
               Where's the new guy?

Shrugs all round.

                         LARA (O.S.)
               I'm so sorry, Sub Fourteen didn't
               make it.

                         THIRTEEN
               Like I said, one by one.

                         KID
               We're all that's left!? What about
               Six.

                         THIRTEEN
               There he is, he's still moving!

Six is still slumped against the ladder. It looks like he is
COUGHING but its the movement from chest compressions -

                         MARCUS
               We need to get him.

                         LARA (O.S.)
               No! We have medics with him now.

INT. GAMERS CIRCLE

A stretcher is carted off. Under the cover is Sub Fourteen.

                         LARA
               We'll update you as soon as we can.

Losing hope she glances back at Six, now on the floor with
the Medics continuing the chest compressions. Standing over
them -

                         NINA
               It's been four minutes. Poor guy.

INT. FLIGHT DECK

Thirteen hits buttons - all doors and bulkheads close and
lock, including the one behind them. On the screen they see
numerous Creatures now isolated.

                         ONE
               So far so good.

                         THIRTEEN
               Nine doors can't shut.

They look at those sectors, the doors are either smashed in
or something is in the way.

                    KID
          They're already getting pissed off.

One shares out bullets between him and Marcus. There are no
more than 20 in total. Marcus gives a handful to Kid -

                    MARCUS
          Hopefully you won't need it.

INT. VARIOUS CORRIDORS AND ROOMS / INT. FLIGHT DECK

As Marcus and One reach doors, they open automatically -
Thirteen is doing this remotely.

                    THIRTEEN (O.S.)
          Hey, I figured out the PA system.

Hyper-aware Marcus is super jumpy.

                    THIRTEEN (O.S.) (CONT'D)
          Take the second door on your right.
          But careful, there's a spider and a
          man - thing.

They enter and it's exactly as described. They FIRE precise
shots.

                    THIRTEEN (O.S.) (CONT'D)
          Ahead of you there's a -
               (trying to find the words)
          - like a wolf, but with more legs.

The sliding bulkhead opens and they see what Thirteen meant
and OPEN FIRE, but it vanishes into the wall to avoid them.

     THIRTEEN (CONT'D)   KID
Ohmygod!   Where'd it go?

Thirteen searches multiple screens, unable to track it down.

INT. GAMERS CIRCLE

Watching Marcus meander cautiously on screen, looking
baffled. The creature nowhere to be seen. Suddenly -

INT. CORRIDOR

                    LARA (O.S.)
          Behind you!

Marcus spins round, FIRES, but after one shot is out of ammo.
He discards that gun and grabs another as the Creature
charges.

To his shock, One's advanced abilities are no more, but his failed parkour move at least draws the Creature's attention. As he lands on his back, it lunges - he FIRES into it's mouth. It falls back in a messy heap.

Marcus helps him up -

                    MARCUS
          You okay?

                    ONE
          Where did that come from?

DISTANT GUNSHOTS ECHO over the PA system!

                    LARA (O.S.)
          Hurry, the others are trapped!

Confused momentarily, Marcus and One hurry towards -

INT. FLIGHT DECK

Thirteen and Kid hide under a controls desk as a MULTI-LIMBED WEIRDO shuffles around erratically when a huge Spider emerges from the wall, rendering their hiding spot futile.

Certain this is the end, Kid's shoulders sag in defeat. One gets there just in time, taking out the Spider but doesn't see the Weirdo behind him. Marcus batters it with his empty weapon in desperation. CLICK-CLICK-CLICK, One's gun is out.

Looking around desperately, One pulls at nearby cables -

                    ONE
          Back up!

Sparks fly as he electrocutes the Weirdo.

Marcus helps Thirteen and Kid to their shaky feet.

INT. A MAZE OF STAIRWELLS AND CORRIDORS

Thirteen leads the way, the gamers keep close together, markedly slower than before. Off One's severe expression -

                    MARCUS
          That was some quick thinking.

                    ONE
          I had no clue it would work.

The corridor splits off, they stop, not knowing which way to turn.

                    LARA (O.S.)
          There's another ladder up ahead.

                    TOM NIKO (O.S.)
          No, they should -

               ONE
          - She's right!

One leads the way.

                    TOM NIKO (O.S.)
          It's easier to -

               LARA (O.S.)
          No! Don't listen -

               ONE
          One speaker please!

                    TOM NIKO (O.S.)
          To the right - I mean left -

               ALL IN THE GAME
          Shut the fuck up Tom!

One turns back and gives Marcus a sly smile. After a moment
of radio SILENCE -

               LARA (O.S.)
          Go up another level -

               THIRTEEN
          But -

               LARA (O.S.)
          Trust me.

They know they can.

INT. TOILET

Humiliated, Tom BURSTS in and kicks a cubicle door, unable to
contain his anger and frustration. Pacing, shaking, sweating -
completely spiralling - he rediscovers some coke in his
pocket. Enters a cubicle for a quick hit to calm his nerves
and boost his confidence.

As he lifts his head in ecstasy he notices the sprinkler
system. His eyes widen at his crazy coke-fuelled idea. From
his other pocket he takes a lighter.

INT. GAMERS CIRCLE

All at once the FIRE ALARM SOUNDS and water jettisons out of
the sprinklers.

INT. INFIRMARY

Everyone cowers in shock covering their ears to no avail.
They all feel the strangest sensations but can't see the
cause, making it all the more frightening.

                    THIRTEEN
          What's happening to us?

Barely able to speak -

                    KID
          I-I-I'm freezing!

                    ONE
          The fire alarm, in the Dome. We
          have to keep going.

EXT. THE DOME - NIGHT

The sound of the ALARM sets off the crowd who go full riot -
pushing, SHOUTING, SCREAMING.

The battle ramps up with more Police arriving in riot gear,
police horses, tear gas, rubber bullets and water cannons.
The Crowd turn on them.

INT. GAMERS CIRCLE

Tom returns to CHAOS. Electrical equipment sparks, smokes and
BLOWS UP, Production Staff try to cover and protect what
equipment they can.

The gamers are still motionless. And drenched.

                    NINA
          Shut it off!

Moments later the water stops.

Tom goes over to Kid, shakes him by the shoulder. No
reaction.

Full of hell -

                    LARA
          This was you, wasn't it!

                    TOM NIKO
          The game has an in-built safety
          override. It stops for alerts like
          fire or carbon monoxide. Or should.

Following Lara's gaze. The game still on. The original rules
no longer apply.

                    TOM NIKO (CONT'D)
                 (under his breath)
          Shit. They're dead.

                    LARA
          Not yet. But you, *you* could have
          electrocuted them. And *us*!

Lara looks down. Marcus shivers in his seat.

INT. LONG, CURVED CORRIDOR

Now being chased by a Wolf-like Creature, the gamers shiver -

                    MARCUS
          I've never been so cold.

Visibly weaker than before. Kid bumps into the others - *as he
is dried off as best as possible in the real world. Their
motionless bodies covered in towels and foil.*

                    KID
          Why can't I just wake up from this
          nightmare?! I can't take much more.

Lagging behind, One turns back to see -

                    ONE
          It's stopped chasing us.
                 (he stops, confused)
          It turned around.

Suddenly, Two Creatures appear ahead of them, merge and
charge. Instinctively the gamers drop into foetal positions
but aren't attacked, but leapt over. As they look up, another
comes bounding around the corner. Marcus pulls them to the
wall.

INT. GAMERS CIRCLE

Production Staff now dry and move equipment. Tom just stands
and watches.

                    TOM NIKO
          Careful! That's expensive
          equipment.

Eyes roll and SIGHS are audible - exasperated by his egotism.
Watching the screens helplessly -

                    NINA
          The game is adapting all the time.

                    TOM NIKO
          Its designed to adjust to keep it
          interesting. And scary.

                         LARA
               Well you succeeded at one thing.

                         NINA
               The AI took that concept and ran
               with it.

                         LARA
                    (talking to Tom)
               It's kid of like *Half-Life Hunter*.
                    (Tom looks at her blankly)
               You know, when Tikonom had to fight
               the - You have no idea what I'm
               talking about do you. You're meant
               to be the brains behind - Have you
               been involved in the making of the
               games at all?

                         TOM NIKO
               I don't have time to oversee
               everything on each individual game.
               Do you realize how big Kagami Games
               is? There's branding, merch, tours,
               interviews -

                         LARA
                    (saddened)
               But you're in charge, you can do
               what you want and pay others to do
               the rest. If you really wanted - If
               you cared about the games -

                         TOM NIKO
               I'm a businessman. You think I'd be
               where I am today if I played video
               games like you sad little nerds!?

Those around him cringe, his true persona revealed to all.
Lara reacts angrily -

                         LARA
               Us 'nerds' paid for those veneers.
               And your botox, and that hideous
               outfit. Rich assholes like you need
               to remember that.

Those close by CLAP in agreement. Tom throws them daggers.

INT. DARK, NARROW CORRIDOR

The gamers race through a door to -

INT. FLIGHT DECK

- and stop dead.

                    MARCUS
          Level 3. I thought we were on 2.

                    ONE
          Me too.

They leave from the same door to -

INT. WIDE, LIT CORRIDOR

Completely different to the last one -

                    MARCUS
          Uh no.

They go through the next door to -

INT. ENGINE ROOM

                    THIRTEEN
          Isn't this -

                    MARCUS
          Level 1.

INT. GAMERS CIRCLE

Nancy dutifully scuttles after Tom, placing an expensive coat
over his shoulders. Lara makes a point of immediately taking
it - places it over Kid. Stunned by the audacity, Tom glowers
at Nancy, who quickly busies herself elsewhere to avoid his
wrath.

                    NINA
          Look!

Pouring over the blueprints -

                    LARA
          It's completely changing the layout
          now.

Pointing to completely different parts of the ship -

                    NINA
          They went from here, to here and -
          Now they're here.

                    TOM NIKO
          That is genius. Why didn't I think
          of that!?

                    NINA
             (to Lara)
          Unbelievable.

Those within earshot shake their heads in disgust.

INT. ENGINE ROOM

Not where they expected to end up yet again. They still
shiver, shuffling on the spot and rub their arms.

                    ONE
          No amount of this will help.

                    THIRTEEN
          You're still doing it though.

Marcus sees an axe. Throws his empty gun down and takes that
instead. One rips a piece of broken pipe from the wall.

                    THIRTEEN (CONT'D)
          What good will they be?

                    MARCUS
          Better than nothing.

The look on Thirteen's face suggests only very slightly.

                    KID
          Who knows what we'll come up
          against next.

                    THIRTEEN
          He should!

                    ONE
          It's altering the difficulty of the
          game. I don't know how.

                    THIRTEEN
          So basically we're *inside* a
          Terminator that is trying to kill
          us.

                    ONE
          It's not a malevolent sentient
          entity. It's a computer program
          that is simply doing what it was
          designed to.

Cold comfort.

                    THIRTEEN
          That's pretty much exactly what *I*
          just said.

                    ONE
          Its M.O. is to keep gameplay up and
          give people a good scare. But not
          to kill. It doesn't understand.

                    THIRTEEN
          And yet -

               KID
          It sorta worked.

                    THIRTEEN
          You hear that Game!? You did your
          job, now let us EXIT GAME! PLEASE!!

INT. SERVER ROOM

Weapons ready. Thirteen and Kid hold their guns like bats.
They eye the walls with as much suspicion and caution as
everything else.

                    THIRTEEN
          It's been too quiet for too long.

                    MARCUS
          Why are we still on the move?
               (off looks)
          The game knows exactly where we
          are. It always does.

Suddenly a snake-like creature BURSTS out of a vent above
Marcus's head. In unison they batter it away.

                    THIRTEEN
          You hurt?

Marcus shakes his head.

                    MARCUS
          I don't think it was even trying to
          attack me.

                    KID
          It's like the game read your mind.
          You said it was too quiet, then
          something came.

                    ONE
          It is.

A new terror crosses their faces.

                    THIRTEEN
          So what's happening is partly our
          fault?

                    ONE
          Try thinking happy thoughts.

                    THIRTEEN
          Are you kidding!?

                    MARCUS
              Lara, how is Six?

INT. GAMERS CIRCLE

Tense SILENCE. The dreaded question. Lara looks over to the
now deserted chair. Only Four left in the circle.

Though loath to break it to them, Lara decides its better
coming from her. Tom reaches for the microphone but she
snatches it away. She takes a moment to compose herself -

                    LARA
              (close to tears)
              We lost him. I'm sorry.

A solemn SILENCE comes over them.

                    ONE (O.S.)
              You shouldn't be sorry.

She looks over at Tom - the one that should.

                    MARCUS (O.S.)
              I wish I hadn't played these stupid
              games so much. I've seen nothing of
              the world. Done nothing else.

                    KID (O.S.)
              Me neither.

Off Marcus's sombre look -

                    ONE
              It's not over yet.

INT. SLEEPING QUARTERS

Still shivering as they enter. There's a SOUND, too faint to
identify. It closes in, GROWS TO A DEAFENING CRESCENDO but
they see nothing. Something dawns on One.

                    MARCUS
              What? What's wrong?

                    ONE
              I think its the Boss Battle!

                    THIRTEEN
              Shit.

Impulsively, they turn back. But find themselves -

INT. MAINTENANCE ROOM

The source of the sound still impossible to locate, yet all
around them. They continue on and end up in -

INT. CARGO HOLD

Weak, tired, cold - the gamers are increasingly sluggish.

Sensing an ambush, One looks over his shoulder to see a huge
skinless Wolf emerge from the wall. From another direction a
SCALY SPIDER and a Weirdo with a multitude of limbs.
Something else materializes from the floor - another Creature
from above.

They merge to form something hideously grotesque. More and
more Creatures materialize, adding to the ever-growing
Creature.

                    MARCUS
          Oh no.

Edging toward the door. They turn and scurry out to -

INT. CARGO HOLD

Face-to-Face with the Boss again, in the exact spot they'd
just left.

                    KID
          No!

The Boss spins around to face them, constantly changing. For
a second it even resembles gamers, as if it absorbed them.

                    MARCUS
          Six!?

INT. GAMERS CIRCLE

                    LARA
          Is this it?

                    TOM NIKO
          Can we give it a targeted virus?

                    NINA
          We can't access the system! At
          all!! What part of impenetrable
          don't you understand!

Lara looks from the insane view on the screen to the gamers
sat helplessly in their chairs, looking so peaceful.

                    LARA
              They're going to -

She can't bring herself to say it out loud. Lara can't stand
to watch - tears out.

EXT. THE DOME - NIGHT

The last few Police and Security still standing are finally
overwhelmed. The crowd PUMMEL the shuttered doors, like a
Creature from the game.

INT. BACKSTAGE

Lara SOBS, pre-mourning her friends when her eyes fall on a
fire axe on the wall. She wipes her eyes and regains her
composure. Studies it - 'in case of emergency, break glass'.

She SMASHES THE GLASS and takes down the axe, much like
Marcus in the game. Her mind reels, eyes dart.

INT. CARGO HOLD

The Boss continues to grow and alter its form. The gamers'
puny weapons will no match. They have barely an ounce of
strength left either. Looking up as if speaking to a God -

                    ONE
              You got nothing?

No answer. Deflated -

                    MARCUS
              This is it.

Marcus looks at One, a recognition passes between them.
Thirteen witnesses the exchange and swallows nervously.

                    THIRTEEN
              I think we could have been friends
              on the outside.

                    MARCUS
              Me too.

Kid can't speak.

Marcus sees the resolve on Thirteen' face. With the last of
his energy -

                    THIRTEEN
              Go, all of you.

With a BELLOW OF RAGE Thirteen charges toward the
shapeshifting Boss. The others look on in shock. Marcus pulls
One and Kid out of harm' way as the Boss turns to pursue him.

INT. CARGO HOLD

They find themselves now at the opposite side.

                    ONE
          My turn.

There's not a hope in hell. Pulling at his arm -

                    MARCUS
          It won't make a difference.

Marcus looks to Kid as One charges forward. Without words,
they come to the same conclusion and bear arms, refusing to
cower in their final moments.

The gamers thrash at the Boss in a last ditch attempt to
survive. It lashes out, sending Marcus flying across the
Cargo Bay. His pain so real.

Kid ducks from a strike as One is grabbed by one of It's many
arms. Kid and Marcus are powerless to help and can only SHOUT
in dismay as One is hoisted high.

Marcus swings the axe again, but it gets stuck in an
appendage and yanked from his grasp. Weaponless, Marcus
stands defiant.

One is stabbed through the torso by an emerging spike as the
Beast constantly morphs into different shapes and creatures.

                    MARCUS (CONT'D)
          Nooo!

Marcus strikes at a spider limb with his bare fists and a
frenzy of frustrated SCREAMING.

With the Boss towering over them and it's many parts reaching
menacingly, Marcus spots up a sharp piece of the creature
chopped off and lying on the floor - bats the spiked
extremity away.

Kid cowers as a spike extremity hurtles toward him.

                    MARCUS (CONT'D)
          Get to the head.

Kid looks up. There are various body parts of a myriad of
creatures all over the Boss.

                    KID
          Which one?

Marcus points to the highest point, the head made from many parts, still distinctive. He hands Kid the extremity.

Looks up and sees his axe still sticking in it. They climb up the Boss, limbs and tails coming out at them from everywhere.

INT. BACKSTAGE

The SOUND FROM OUTSIDE is louder, closer.

Lara's eyes fall on a large electricity cable running up the wall behind her.

INT. CARGO HOLD

Marcus reaches the axe. Chops as he goes as if climbing Mount Everest. Kid already at the head, stabs it in the eye with its own appendage to satisfying effect. Marcus swings the axe at the neck.

INT. BACKSTAGE

                    LARA
          I'm so sorry Marcus.

Before she loses her nerve, she swings the axe at the cable. Sparks fly then - DARKNESS.

INT. AUDITORIUM

The SOUND OF PANIC as everything goes black.

EXT. DOME - NIGHT

The crowd go QUIET in the sudden darkness.

EXT. CITY BLOCKS - NIGHT

Block by block the darkness spreads.

INT. GAMERS CIRCLE

Lara enters to torchlight flitting in all directions and the BUZZ OF CONFUSION. She moves towards -

                    THREE
          Did you do this!?

She pushes past him, doesn't react. It's hard to see. She fumbles over to Marcus. His chair empty. Shocked, Lara turns toward Kid's chair - he's alive!

Tears in her eyes, she reaches out to help him up - groggy,
stiff and shivering. On the other side of him is --

                    LARA
               (stunned)
          Marcus. You're okay!!?

Lara pulls Marcus in for a hug. Marcus returns it.

INT. BACKSTAGE

A torch is shone on the axe still wedged in the cable on the
wall. Eyebrows are raised.

INT. GAMERS CIRCLE

Lara spots the device still in Marcus's ear and throws it on
the floor. Kid stomps on it, and his own.

               MARCUS   LARA
How?   How?

They don't care, and hug some more. As Kid watches on, Lara
pulls him in too.

                    LARA
          Brian, nice to finally meet you!

Kid and Marcus exchange looks - *How does she know?* Lara
simply WINKS.

                    TOM NIKO
          That was some luck, right!?

                    LARA
          No thanks to you.

                    TOM NIKO
          It's terrible, what you went
          through. There's only one of these,
               (an award in his hands)
          but I'll get another made special.

Marcus won't take it. Kid reaches to instead, but lets it
slip through his hands and SMASH to pieces at Tom's feet.

Out of nowhere, a fist knocks Tom backwards to the floor -
Kid's Dad. Witnesses CLAP and CHEER nearby. Kid leaps to
embrace him. LAUGHING with pure joy is Nina -

                    TOM NIKO (CONT'D)
          You're -

                    NINA
          - I quit!

                    KID'S DAD
          What'd I say, never meet your
          heroes.

INT. BACKSTAGE AT PRESS CONFERENCE - DAY

                    LARA
          Are you nervous?

Marcus shakes his head. Smiles. Shows her a letter -

                    LARA (CONT'D)
          Sponsorship! You are going pro!?

Marcus nods.

                    LARA (CONT'D)
          But what about our -

                    MARCUS
          Gaming can wait a year. I'm already
          packed.

OVER THE FOLLOWING SCENES -

                    ANNOUNCER
          Following Mr. Niko being charged
          with the involuntary manslaughter
          of eleven gamers, and his game and
          device being permanently shelved,
          we have been in desperate need for
          a new hero. But instead we got
          three. Please welcome Brian Grant,
          Lara Fisher and Marcus Gordon.

INT. BUSY NEWSAGENT

Headlines include - Endless Terror for Troubled Games
Company, Alien Mind Game Fails to Launch. There are also
headlines like - The True Heroes of Dome Terror (with
pictures of Marcus, Brian and Lara).

People recognize Marcus - point and take pictures. He doesn't
let it bother him.

INT. PASSENGER BOARDING BRIDGE - NIGHT

Lara and Marcus walk through the long, narrow corridor.

SEAT BELT

Pulled secure as ENGINES ROAR.

SEATS RATTLE

As Lara takes Marcus by the hand in the middle of a
commercial flight during take-off.

INT. PRESS CONFERENCE ON A KID'S TV

Marcus and Brian take a seat as cameras flash.

                         ANNOUNCER
             Questions?

Every hand reaches up in eagerness.

                                        CUT TO BLACK /
                                        FADE FROM BLACK:

EXT. HALLSTATT, AUSTRIA - DAY

A boat on the water in a spectacular landscape. Marcus and
Lara step on, backpacks in tow. They take in the remarkable
natural beauty of the place. Eye contact.

                                        CUT TO BLACK.

www.ingramcontent.com/pod-product-compliance
Lightning Source LLC
Chambersburg PA
CBHW071925120726
48001CB00005B/1879